Just One Dare

The Dirty Dares
Book 1

NEW YORK TIMES BESTSELLING AUTHOR
Carly Phillips

JUST ONE DARE

One night. No names. No expectations—but *un*expected consequences.

I never thought I'd see my daughter's father again, but six years later I come face to face with Nick Dare, an irresistible man with demands of his own.

But I'm no longer that desperate girl sleeping in the back room of a diner. I'm part of the illustrious Kingston family, a successful businesswoman, and I'm raising a little girl who is my world. My life is steady. Controlled. Safe at last.

Until Nick Dare walks back in with billionaire, boss energy. The man who once ruined me for anyone else. He wants answers and he *says* he wants us.

But letting him in means risking everything—my heart and the life I've fought so hard to build.

And Nick? He's not stopping until he has it all.

CHAPTER ONE

Aurora

S TANDING IN FRONT of the bathroom mirror, I put the finishing touches on my lipstick and step back to look at my handiwork. I barely recognize the woman staring back at me. Six years ago, I was pregnant and homeless, with no idea what the next day would bring.

Now I'm wearing a sleeveless, cream-colored, satin gown with a strapless neckline, draped corset bodice, and an actual train, sent over by the designer, himself. A limousine waits outside to take me to Lincoln Center for a movie premiere. I curled my hair in long waves and applied makeup, doing my best to look as glamorous as possible for my evening with famous stars the average person will never meet.

This is my life and there are moments, like now, when I still have to pinch myself to be sure I'm not dreaming.

"Mommy, look! I'm going with you to the party tonight!" My five-year-old daughter Leah stomps into the room wearing a pink, sparkly princess gown from her dress-up box, with matching shoes that are too big for her little feet and a handbag dangling from her arm. "Makeup please!" Leah closes her eyes and puckers her lips, making her *I'm ready* face.

I laugh. My daughter is such a little diva, I think, as I pick up the tube of gloss and swiped it over Leah's tiny pursed lips. "All set. You look beautiful!"

"I know!" Leah says with confidence that never ceases to amaze me. "So do you, Mommy."

"Thank you, honey." Smiling, I reach out and tug on Leah's long blonde hair that is still damp from her bath. It curls around her adorable face.

I see my own features in my daughter's smaller ones, but I also catch glimpses of Leah's father in my child, at least, in the unique indigo color of his eyes.

It was a sizzling Florida summer. Nick was visiting a friend who lived in Miami Beach. It was the same day I turned eighteen and aged out of foster care. I had nowhere to go except the diner where I worked and I was lucky the owners allowed me to stay in the back room.

While serving tables that afternoon, I met Nick-we exchanged first names only—and we spent one night together. It was incredible…and enough to result in me getting pregnant. But at the time? The hours I spent with Nick on the beach and later in his hotel room were an unexpected, and pleasurable, escape from the painful reality of my life.

As usual, when I think of my daughter's father, a pang of regret hits me hard. Without Nick's last name, I had no way to find him once I discovered I was pregnant. Although Leah would never know her daddy, I console myself with the fact that my daughter has uncles who will stand in as father figures and male role models.

Men I would never have met, if my oldest half-brother, Linc, hadn't managed to uncover my existence after our father, the bastard, passed away. When going through our father's things, Linc discovered checks that Kenneth Kingston sent as payment to keep me out of his life and in foster care.

Linc traveled to Florida, where I grew up, welcomed me into the family, and remained in town long enough to get to know me. And he allowed me the time to decide if I wanted to move to New York and be part of their clan.

Leah slides her hand into mine. "Let's go to the ball!" she cries out in a high-pitched voice, pulling me out of my musings about the past, and things I can't change.

"Honey, you know Samantha is babysitting tonight."

The girl is a high-school senior who lives in the neighborhood and occasionally watches Leah so I can get work done.

"I know," Leah says with a dramatic sigh. She releases my hand, steps out of the bathroom and begins to spin around the bedroom. "But I'd rather meet my handsome prince tonight. Are you going to meet *your* handsome prince at the ball, Mommy?" Ever since we watched *Cinderella*, Leah has been obsessed with the idea of finding her prince.

She keeps spinning, saving me from having to answer. There haven't been any princes in my life—handsome or otherwise—since the night I got pregnant.

I watch as Leah pretends to dance across the ballroom floor. Samantha is going to have a rough time getting Leah to sleep unless she puts on a quiet movie to chill her out first. She twirls around, nearly missing the dresser as she spins.

"Stop before you get dizzy or trip!" I say, too late.

Thanks to her play shoes, Leah's feet get tangled and she ends in a heap on the floor, giggling.

I sigh. "Come on. Up you go." I help my daughter stand. "Time to go downstairs and wait for your sitter."

"I like Samantha. Do you think she'd play Barbies with me? I want to show her Malibu Barbie and Ken. He promised to take Barbie to the ball tonight, too!"

A grin pulls at my lips. "I'm sure she'll play whatever you want before bed but remember, you promised to be good for her." I grab my purse from the bed where I left it and lead Leah downstairs just as the doorbell rings.

"Samantha!" Leah barrels the rest of the way down the stairs. Thank goodness she left her dress-up shoes on the floor in the bedroom.

"Remember, don't open the door until I get there!" I call out. Leah has a bad habit of forgetting the *'Don't open the door without a grown-up present'* rule.

I reach the door where Leah is hopping in excitement, but she hasn't unlocked it or let Samantha inside. "Thank you for listening. Now what do we do?" I ask.

"Who is it?" Leah yells loudly.

"It's Samantha!" the babysitter says back.

Smiling, I nodded at my daughter. "Go ahead."

Leah reaches up, turns the lock, and opens the front door. "Samantha! Let's play!" she says before the girl can even step inside.

The pretty teen laughs and edges her way into the house.

I glance at Leah. "Let me go over everything with Samantha before I leave. Go change into your pajamas, and Samantha will be right in."

"Okay, Mommy."

"First, give me kiss good night." Ignoring my

gown, I bend down and bask in the warmth and sweetness of Leah's arms around my neck. "Night, sweetheart."

"Good night, Mommy." Leah turns and runs for her room.

Samantha stands, waiting. "You look pretty, Ms. Kingston."

"Thank you. It should be a fun night. I'm guessing I'll be home around one, like we discussed."

"No problem. I drove my mom's car." The neighborhood with free-standing houses is well-lit and safe. Samantha only lives about four houses down, but I still feel better if she has her SUV or gets picked up instead of walking home after dark. I can't leave a sleeping Leah to drive Samantha home myself.

"Great." I go over Leah's bedtime routine and schedule, what she can and cannot eat—no matter what she claims—and confirm that Samantha has my cell phone number.

I walk out the front door and wait until I hear the lock turn behind me, before heading down the steps and towards the limousine waiting to take me from Long Island to Manhattan.

I've been a Kingston for the last five years, but I'll never get used to the perks that come with being wealthy and part of a famous family.

As the limo takes me into the city, I can't help

thinking of the family I knew nothing about for most of my life.

Linc is the CEO of Kingston Enterprises, a real-estate company worth millions. Linc is married to Jordan, his best friend and the woman who accompanied him to meet me for the first time. The premiere I'm attending stars famous actress Sasha Keaton, my sister-in-law, and world-renowned actor, Harrison Dare. The film was acquired by K-Talent Productions, a company owned by Sasha, Harrison, and Xander, Sasha's husband and my half-brother.

It should be an incredible premiere. There is already Oscar buzz surrounding the film and the performances.

Adding to the fairy dust that was sprinkled over my life, the film's producer, Cassidy Kingston, is married to my brother, Dash, the lead singer of the world-famous rock band, The Original Kings. Rounding out my family is another real estate mogul, Beck Daniels, Linc's former nemesis, who is now married to my half-sister, Chloe.

All in all, I have four half siblings. And their mother, Melly, stepped in to act as a surrogate mom to me and grandmother to Leah.

Not only did I go from poverty to immense wealth, but I also went from being totally alone to suddenly being a part of a family filled with warm, kindhearted people. And that is what really matters. I wouldn't care if the Kingstons were dirt poor. The love and security they've given me is priceless.

The limousine pulls up to the red carpet, and the driver opens my door. I step out and as promised, Xander is waiting to walk me in at the drop-off point.

"You look beautiful," he says, leaning in and pressing a kiss to my cheek.

I look at my screenwriter brother in his tuxedo and black-framed eyeglasses, and grin. "You look pretty hot yourself. Eyes bothering you? Headache?" I ask, worried whenever he has his glasses on.

During a stint in the Marines, his unit was hit by an IED. He suffered a head injury, leading to issues that resulted in his medical discharge. He only wears his glasses when he works late or is suffering from dizziness or headaches.

"I'm fine. I was up late writing, that's all."

I study him, taking in his coloring and expression and decide he is telling the truth. "How's Sasha?" I ask.

"Excited. Gorgeous." He lights up at the subject of his wife. "I hope this movie is the one that earns her an Oscar."

"You're so cute." I grin. "Thanks for meeting me." I didn't have to walk the red carpet, but my brothers know of my insecurities and take good care of me.

I enter the room, doing my best not to let my jaw drop or show my overwhelming awe at seeing so many famous and beautiful people surrounding me. This is the pre-screening, and we'll be ushered into the theater area soon.

"I see Dash and Cassidy," I say to Xander. "Go find your wife." I pat his arm and send him on his way. "Dash, Cassidy!" I call, catching their attention before they can get lost in the crowd.

They turn and I walk over, joining them. Cassidy is nine months pregnant, due any day now, and glowing despite her large belly.

"Who's watching the princess?" Cassidy asks.

I slide my hair over one shoulder. "I have a babysitter who lives in the neighborhood. If Leah doesn't wear her out and she's willing to come back next time I need her, I consider it a win." I'm still reeling from watching my daughter's antics as I got ready.

Dash laughs. "Maybe she'll play guitar for her all night?"

"Funny," I mutter, at his reference to the guitar he bought Leah last year for Christmas. I gave him hell.

Especially after Leah started waking me up at five every morning when she played. Badly. The child does not take after her talented uncle when it comes to music—at least, not yet. She is young, and there is time, but until she's older, I have no intention of spending money on lessons. I need Leah to have a burning desire to learn before that point. Right now, she's just a little girl who tends to jump from one thing to another.

I decide to change the subject. "I cannot wait to see the film!"

Cassidy's cheeks turn red, no doubt because it is her first solo turn at producing. "I'm so nervous," she says. "I'm not sure if the twisting in my stomach is the baby or anxiety!" She rubs her lower back, and I glance at her with concern.

"Babe, you've got this. They're already talking Oscar and Golden Globe nominations. I'm so proud of you." Dash hugs her to his side.

Watching them, I feel a twinge of envy at the wonderful relationships my siblings found. Though I am beyond happy for each of them, I can't seem to get past the struggle my life was before Linc found me. And now, my focus has to be on Leah. Any man interested in me will find out Leah and I are a package deal. Leah will always come first with me. And I am determined to shower my girl with all the love and security I never had growing up.

"Don't remind me," Cassidy says of the potential awards, still holding on to her belly in a way that does not make me comfortable.

"Are you feeling okay?" I ask.

"I am." Cassidy blows out a breath and seems to shake off whatever she's feeling. "I'm just tired. We made the rounds when we arrived."

"That's why we found a place to hide out in for a little while," Dash adds, glancing around the corner where they stand.

I nod. "I remember how tough it was at the end of my pregnancy. You should get off your feet and rest."

"She's right," Dash says, his growing concern also obvious by the tight expression on his face.

Cassidy sighs. "Soon." She looks around the room, and her gaze settles on an area near the bar. "Looks like Harrison's family is as close as yours."

I met Harrison Dare when Sasha, Xander and Cassidy were just starting to put their production company together. Dash and Xander have houses in East Hampton, and since I was staying with Melly, I went to visit often. With Sasha and Cassidy's help, I managed to set up a nonprofit organization very close to my heart—one that helps girls and boys who age out of foster care start their new lives on the right foot.

Harrison, who I recognize in the group, is a true movie star. He is irresistible, with his thick black hair, and sexy smile that is just short of perfect, courtesy of one side tooth that overlaps another, but which only adds to his appeal. Right now, he is surrounded by men I don't know. One has his back to me, and the others are obviously related, given their similar features.

"The Dirty Dares." I grin at the name Harrison uses to describe his family. It is also on their Dirty Dare vodka brand.

"Yes. Their vodka is world famous and extremely good. I wish I could have a drink before I have to sit through an hour and a half of waiting for everyone to watch the first movie I produced," Cassidy says with a cute whine.

"The doctor says you can have a small glass of white wine," Dash says, in a *don't push your luck* tone of voice.

I am about to pull my gaze away from the huddle of handsome men when the one whose face I couldn't see turns my way. Familiarity hits me in the gut.

But there is no possible way it is him. I was thinking about Leah's father earlier, and he was on my mind. That is the only reason I think Nick is standing across the room from me now.

Of course, the rationale doesn't stop my stomach from spasming or my palms from sweating. Then he looks at me head on, those eyes I was musing on earlier meeting mine.

"Oh, my God." My voice shakes and dizziness assaults me.

Cassidy glances over.

"What's wrong?" Dash immediately clasps my elbow and pulls me toward him, protective as usual.

I shake my head. "Nothing… I… There's someone who looks familiar but…" *It can't be him. What are the odds?*

But he's already left the other men and has started towards me. I panic. I need…time to think, to breathe, to accept who he is and what finding him here means.

"I…I need the ladies' room!" I jerk my arm out of Dash's grip and bolt for the double doors that lead to a hallway where the bathrooms are located.

"Aurora?" Chloe calls out my name as I pass my sister by, not stopping to talk. But I feel my sister's presence as Chloe follows me to the ladies' room.

I don't care as long as I have a few minutes to process one very important fact. Nick, my daughter's father, is here. And my entire life is about to change. Again.

★ ★ ★

Nick

I STAND WITH my brothers, killing time until we're let into the theater to see Harrison's latest movie. I do my best to keep my attention on the conversation around me, but it's hard. Yesterday I was in L.A., overseeing an issue in one of our California Meridian hotels. Tonight, I'm in Manhattan, trying to keep my eyes open.

My siblings and I wear tuxedos, all except Zach, who insists on marching to his own beat, which, in this case, means he is dressed in dark jeans, a hooded leather jacket, and scuffed, black motorcycle boots. Ever the rebel. The only person missing is my twin sister, Jade, for reasons everyone understands. She suffers from migraines and isn't feeling well, though I sense the reason she skipped tonight go deeper than that. I'll have to talk to her about it tomorrow.

"I thought you were bringing a date?" Asher, my oldest sibling, says, interrupting my thoughts. "One of the women you know in the city." He takes a sip of his vodka as he waits for an answer.

At the question, I rethink my decision not to drink tonight, but I figure the alcohol won't help my jet lag.

"Umm, no. Last woman I was with used up her three dates," I say.

Harrison groans. "You really are an asshole."

I shake my head, disagreeing. "If I let a relationship go on, knowing it doesn't have a chance, then I'd be the asshole who led the woman on." I shrug. "In three dates, I pretty well know if something's going to work out or not. Seems fair to me."

Zach bursts out laughing. "Are you still using that rule?"

"It's a solid one." As far as I'm concerned, a woman's true personality isn't difficult to discern. Especially when money is involved. Women who are after me for the Dare name or fortune usually show their true colors quickly.

I ignore my brothers' comments and turn to look around. Thanks to Harrison's talent and fame, I'm used to premieres, after parties and mixing with celebrities around the room.

My gaze lands on Dash Kingston, lead singer of The Original Kings, and one of my favorite rock bands. We met earlier when Harrison introduced Dash's very pregnant wife as the producer of tonight's film. Beside him stands a blonde woman with a knockout body in a gorgeous fitted gown.

A surge of awareness ripples through me. But it isn't one of simple attraction, though I am definitely drawn to her. It's something more. I continue to stare until, as if sensing the weight of my gaze, she turns her head.

Her eyes widen, and I realize I'm right. What I feel is a renewed connection with the only woman with whom I ever experienced something real. I might have been young then but I *knew*.

I'm halfway across the room before I register that

I've moved. Though people block my way, I manage to catch sight of her rushing out the double doors. So, I follow.

I reach the hallway just as she disappears into the Ladies' Room. I have no doubt she recognizes me, but I don't understand why she ran. We had one amazing night together. Why would that freak her out now?

Determined to get an answer, I prop myself against the wall outside the bathroom door and settle in to wait. Aurora—no last names needed—got away from me once before.

I'm not about to let it happen again.

★   ★   ★

Aurora

I SIT IN a chair in the outer room of the restroom, attempting to pull myself together.

"Breathe," Chloe says, putting a hand on my back.

"Trying." My mind is spinning. Nick is here! I thought I'd never see him again.

Shortly after our time together, I found myself pregnant and alone. Then Braden and Willow Prescott, whom I met at the free clinic where I went for prenatal care in Florida, gave me a place to stay. And not long after that, Linc showed up and told me I was a

Kingston. And though I was no longer been alone, through it all, I was a *single mother*. It's the way I identify myself, then and now. And I didn't expect that to change.

But now Leah's father has surfaced, and questions filter through my brain. Will Nick want to be part of his daughter's life? Will he fight for custody? Is that possible? I don't know him at all—not really. There is one thing I am certain of, though—things are going to change. At the thought, I begin hyperventilating again.

"Okay enough." Chloe gets down on her knees. "You need to tell me what's going on, because I'm starting to panic."

"I… Okay. I just…"

"Let's start with why you ran out of the ballroom." Now that she has my attention, Chloe's voice gentles.

I nod and pull in a longer breath. "I saw someone from my past."

Chloe places a hand on my knee, steadying herself. "Who?"

Tears fill my eyes, but I refuse to let them fall. "Leah's father," I whisper.

"Holy shit! No wonder you're in here hyperventilating!" Chloe pushes herself up. "Sorry, I have to stand. This position is killing my knees." Then she looks at me and sighs. "Do you want to tell me how you met him?"

I never discussed that night with my family. It never seemed to matter. After all, I couldn't track Nick down, no matter how much money I now have.

"It was my birthday. I had aged out of foster care that day, and I'd gone to work at the diner, as usual. I'd already made arrangements with the owners—they'd agreed to let me sleep in the back room, thank God," I say, recalling my past. "I waited on a table of guys. One of them—his name was Nick—asked me out that night. Normally, I'd have said no, but it was my birthday and I figured I deserved something good that day…" I trail off, remembering.

I was attracted to Nick from the moment I saw him. The other guys around the table were cocky, prep-school types. Most had blond hair and sticks up their asses. They whistled and winked at me, but they were just showing off for their friends.

Nick was different. Kinder. Confident in an innate way. He didn't have to prove himself or act superior. He was just a hot, sexy guy who knew what he wanted. I couldn't believe he chose me.

Chloe waits patiently for me to continue.

I draw a deep breath. "We had dinner, walked on the beach and talked, a lot. We ended up back in his room and…you know the rest. But he used protection." I wave my hands in the air, as frustrated now as I was then. "It was just one of those freak things."

I never regretted having Leah. I adore my child. Leah is my life. But at the time, my fear was overwhelming.

"Nick and I never exchanged last names. We both knew he was in town for a short time visiting a friend, and that he'd go back to his life. And I had to figure out mine."

"But now he's out there?" Chloe asks.

"He was standing with the so-called Dirty Dare brothers."

Chloe narrows her gaze. "You said Nick." She pulls her phone from her purse. "Don't worry. I'm just asking Sasha if there's a Nick Dare." Her fingers tap on the screen.

I blink. "He looked like Harrison," I whisper.

A few seconds later, Chloe's phone beeps and she glances down. "And we have a winner. Nick Dare is your baby daddy."

I nod slowly. A Dare. A cousin to Dr. Braden Prescott and his wife, Willow, who helped me when I was pregnant.

Well, that is a coincidence, but it is one I can handle. Nick being here, now, will be harder.

"I have to face him. He needs to know about Leah." My insides tremble at the thought.

Chloe sighs. "He does. But why don't you start with just seeing him again, then go from there. Can you do that?"

"I have no choice." Drawing a deep breath for courage, I rise to my feet. Though I am mortified that I ran away like a coward, I needed time to get over the shock.

It is time to face my past.

"I'm ready," I say to Chloe.

My sister pulls me into a hug—something that even after five years, I am still getting used to, after a lifetime deprived of affection.

I hug Chloe back. "Thank you."

"Don't be silly. That's what family is for." Chloe shoots me a look, and I nod.

Chloe steps towards the bathroom door and walks outside, and I follow behind. But I don't have to go far.

Just as I step out into the hallway, I come face to face with Nick.

CHAPTER TWO

Nick

ARMS FOLDED ACROSS my chest, I wait, leaning against the wall in the small hallway. My patience is wearing thin and I am *this* close to barging into the Ladies' Room when the woman who followed Aurora inside steps out, with Aurora right behind her.

I push myself up and block her escape. Up close, her porcelain skin looks pale and those blue eyes seem a little too large in her face. But she is still gorgeous. She's grown up, filled out in all the best ways, and looking at her knocks me on my ass.

"Nick."

My name, coming from those glossed lips, does something to me. "So, you remember me."

She swallows hard and glances at her friend. "I'm okay, Chloe. You can go find Beck. I'll look for you after Nick and I talk."

Chloe, an attractive blonde—though not as pretty as Aurora, at least in Nick's eyes—gives him a long, assessing look. "Okay. But you know your brothers are all here if you need them," she says, her gaze never leaving mine. Clearly that comment is for my benefit. A warning, not to hurt Aurora.

Wait a minute. Brothers? Aurora told me she was an only child.

Chloe strides off, leaving us alone.

"So…this is a shock." Her hands twist around her small purse, showing her nervousness.

"I came back to the diner to see you." I believe in getting right to the point.

After she left my room all those years ago, I tried to convince myself that what we shared was nothing more than one special night. But I couldn't let her go. I was drawn to her in a way I couldn't explain. So, I showed up at the diner where we met a couple of hours later, only to have another server inform me that it was her day off. I left with a weight in my gut, knowing I was getting on a plane at six a.m. the next morning, and it was likely I would never see her again.

"I know," she says softly. "I thought it was best if we didn't get any further involved." She glances away, obviously finding it hard to meet my gaze.

As realization dawns, my gut begins to churn. "You were there and didn't want to see me."

She tips her head, acknowledging the truth. "It was only supposed to be one night, and my life was more complicated than I let on."

I groan, understanding her reasoning even if I hate

the truth. "Then tell me now." I want to understand what cost us all these years.

She draws a deep breath and lets it out slowly. "We do need to talk, Nick, but the movie is going to start soon, and I can't miss it. A lot of my family members are involved in the production."

"So is my brother," I say. "Which brings me to another question. You told me you had no family." Did she lie and if so, *why*? And did she lie about anything else?

"I didn't. At least, not until Linc Kingston came to find me. Look, it's a very long story and I *will* tell you. Just not now."

Patience isn't my strong suit, but I have to agree with her, especially once the lights begin flashing, indicating we are to head into the theater.

I reach into my pocket and pull out my cell. "Give me your number," I say, handing it to her. No way will I rely on her calling me.

She accepts the phone and inputs her number.

I take it back and immediately hit send, causing a ring to sound from her purse.

"You don't trust me?" she asks, her eyes open wide.

I can't control the smirk that crosses my lips. "Just not taking any chances of losing you again." I wink at her and walk off, leaving her to think about the possibilities of our reunion.

I'll be doing the same. No way will I be able to pay attention to whatever is happening on the big screen in front of me. Even if my brother's ugly mug is front and center.

★   ★   ★

Aurora

I WALK INTO the theater and stride toward the front row, where my family is seated. But instead of everyone settling in to watch the movie, the Kingstons are in a group, talking excitedly.

"Chloe? What's going on?" I ask, joining them.

"Cassidy's water broke! She went into labor and Dash rushed her to the hospital." Her eyes are dancing with excitement.

"What is everyone going to do? How can they choose whether to stay or go to the hospital?" I ask.

"Nobody's leaving this theater," Linc says, obviously having heard my question. "I promised Dash we'd stay for Sasha. And Cassidy produced the movie. We owe it to her to watch. Besides, she'll be in labor for a while. We can go to the hospital afterwards."

"The King has spoken," I say, laughing. Linc is the nominal head of the family and we all recognize it.

Once Kenneth Kingston was gone—and from what I understand, even before—everyone deferred to Linc. And I do, too. I owe him, I love him, and I appreciate his wisdom.

He shakes his head at me and chuckles before turning back to Jordan.

"Are you okay?" Chloe asks me quietly.

I nod. "But I would like to talk."

"You got it. I'm going to the hospital after the movie ends. I assume you need to get home for the babysitter?" Chloe asks. Unlike me, Chloe and Beck have a live-in nanny, so if they need to stay out later, they can.

"Yes. But I'll go see Cass, Dash and the baby to-morrow."

Despite the upheaval of seeing Nick and the antic-ipation of the new baby, I manage to enjoy the movie. I am so proud of my family members' accomplish-ment, and tell them. They depart immediately after the film, even Sasha, the star, rushing to the hospital. Family first is the Kingston motto, and it settled in my heart the moment I learned I was a part of this won-derful group of people.

Still, I can't wait to get home, wanting nothing more than to see my little girl's face and listen to her soft breaths as she sleeps. At least I bought myself some time to think before I have to deal with Nick.

He'll call me when he's ready to talk, and we can set a time to meet. And before then, I'll be able to get Chloe's advice.

Once I walk into the house, I pay Samantha, then watch her get into her car safely and pull out of the driveway. Blowing out a breath, I lock the door, set the alarm, and walk upstairs. I peeked into Leah's room and see my little girl's body asleep in her bed. Without letting myself overthink or panic—yet—I go to my own room to undress, wash up, and put on a comfortable t-shirt.

Needing to be close to my daughter, I walk back to Leah's room, then place my phone on the nightstand and slide into the double bed beside my daughter. The scent of Leah's familiar shampoo gives me a sense of security I desperately need tonight. Seeing Nick brings forth a host of emotions I'm not sure how to handle—everything from remembering the wonder of our night together, to fearing what the disruption of having a father in Leah's life will mean, to panic about custody issues and who knows what else. I wrap an arm around my daughter and eventually drift to sleep.

A short time later—I'm not sure just *how* long—the jarring sound of my phone ringing rouses me, and I grab it before Leah awakes. Not that I have to worry. My daughter can sleep through a hurricane.

I slide out of bed, answering as I walk into the hall.

"Hello?"

"It's a boy!" Chloe exclaims. "Ask me his name."

I laugh. "What's his name?"

"Freddie Kingston. They named him after Freddie Mercury."

Rolling my eyes, I smile. "Of course our brother, the rock star, named his kid after his idol. How's Cass?"

"Doing well. I think they'll send her home late tomorrow. So if you can't make it to the hospital, you can visit once they're settled," Chloe says.

"I'll call in the morning and see what they'd prefer. Thanks for letting me know. And if you're still there, send my love." I will text both Dash and Cassidy after we hang up. I'll spare them the phone call tonight, knowing how exhausted Cass must be.

"Will do. Are *you* okay?" Chloe asks, obviously referring to me having seen Nick tonight.

I sigh. "I am. Don't worry. We'll talk tomorrow," I assure my sister, not wanting to worry her.

"Okay. Love you. Night." Chloe disconnects the call.

I push thoughts of Nick aside, text the new parents and walk back into the room to catch some more sleep. Tomorrow will come soon enough and with it, Nick Dare.

★   ★   ★

Nick

I ATTEND THE after-party for the film and am surprised to find none of the Kingstons there, until Harrison tells me Cassidy Kingston went into labor. That explains why they all disappeared, Aurora included.

"Hey, man. What's going on? You've seemed off all night," Harrison says, ever the observant actor.

Despite his fame, Harrison is as down-to-earth as they come. He has to be, in order to survive in our big family where everyone is treated equally and open to the same amount of ribbing, no matter their occupation or status. Looking out for one another always comes first.

I take a sip of tequila, having given in to the need for a drink. No, I wasn't imbibing in the family vodka. I want something harsher.

"Do you remember when I went to visit a friend in Miami Beach after my sophomore year of college?" I ask my sibling.

My brother leans against the high-top table, a puzzled look on his face. "Vaguely."

"I met a girl there." Then I go on to explain my night with Aurora, our 'no last name' agreement, me falling for her and going back the next morning, only to have to leave the state before catching up with her again. "I never thought I'd see her again but she was here tonight. And you won't believe who she is."

Harrison raises his brows. "You gonna tell me?"

"Aurora Kingston."

He blinks, his surprise etched all over his face. "You're kidding?"

"No." I wouldn't make up such a close connection to our family.

"Did you talk to her tonight?"

I groan. "I tried. She panicked and ran, but we managed to have a brief talk. I got her phone number, so I won't lose her again."

"Hmm. Mr. Three Dates and it's over? What's your plan with this girl? And before you answer, you'd better think long and hard because she's Xander's sister and Sasha's sister-in-law. *My partners*, if your brain hasn't kicked into gear yet," Harrison reminds me.

I roll my eyes. "I'm not an idiot. I wouldn't go after her if my intentions weren't…" Fuck. What *are* my intentions?

This is a woman I met six years ago. I barely knew her then but even so, I wanted to understand more about what made her tick and why we clicked. And after one look at her tonight, I still do.

"Don't worry, okay?"

Harrison studies me, his eyes narrowing. "You said the summer after your sophomore year. That was what? Six years ago?"

I nod. "Why?"

My brother shakes his head. "No reason. So, what are your plans, as far as seeing her?"

I finish my drink and place the glass on the table. "I was going to call and set up a date. But the more I think about her reaction to me tonight, the more I realize I can't give her the chance to refuse. I think I'm going to find her address and simply show up at her house. That way, she'll have to talk to me." I lean closer to my brother. "Any chance you can get me her address from your partners?"

Downing the last of his drink, Harrison shakes his head. "What makes you think they'll share their sister's address with me?"

"Because you can be the most persuasive human in the world when you want to be." I wait in silence, giving my brother time to think about it. With Harrison, I find it's better to wait him out than annoy him to death.

"Fine. But you owe me." He pulls out his phone just as his agent strides over.

"Can I have a word?" the man asks.

Harrison nods. "I'll call Xander as soon as we're

done," he says to me. "You know, sometimes when you revisit the past, you uncover surprises you don't expect."

"Is that another warning, big brother?"

Harrison shakes his head. "Just stating a fact. I'll be in touch."

"Thanks." I slap Harrison on the back.

Knowing my brother will come through, I leave the party and head to the Meridian hotel—the place I call home when in New York. Hotel living isn't for everyone but I don't mind. Having room and maid service fits my current bachelor lifestyle and since I travel so much for work, the situation suits me.

Once in my room, I strip out of the monkey suit I wore tonight and crash in bed. Unfortunately, sleep won't come. Not while I wait for Harrison to call with the address that, I have a hunch, will change my life.

Aurora

"MOMMY. MOMMY. MOMMY. Mommy!"

I wake up to find Leah leaning over me, shaking my shoulders.

"Sorry, honey. I fell asleep late." I push myself up and sit back against the headboard, waiting for my mind to clear.

"You slept in my bed!" Leah claps her hands and her words bring back last night's shock. I saw Nick and now I need to prepare myself for what comes next—dealing with Leah's father.

I know nothing about Nick. Does he have a wife? A girlfriend? Someone I will have to share my daughter with? Nausea fills me, but I push it away. I am not a homeless teen anymore, with no money or support. I am an adult with an equally powerful family behind me. And I am far from penniless—I even have a trust fund in my name, thanks to my siblings all agreeing that I deserved to inherit as much as they did from our father's passing. I possess more confidence than I did years ago, and am as protective as a mama bear when it comes to my daughter.

I turn my focus back to Leah who sits waiting for me to reply. "I did sleep in your bed. I wanted cuddles." I tickle Leah until her giggles and shrieks echo around the room, and only stop so Leah can catch her breath. "Now why did you wake me?"

Leah presses her hands on either side of my cheeks. "I want pancakes!" she yells.

"Indoor voice." I smile. "I could go for pancakes too." Why let nausea get the best of me when I can eat my troubles away, at least temporarily? "Let me go to my room and I'll be down in a few minutes. You go to your bathroom and go potty, then brush your teeth, okay?"

"Okay, Mommy. Can I have chocolate chips in my pancakes?" Leah bats her lashes like a pro, causing me to laugh.

"Good try. You had ice cream with Samantha last night. That was your treat." The babysitter filled me in on their fun-filled night.

"Fine," Leah says with a huff. "Then can I stir the mix?"

I ruffle her hair. "Yeah. You can."

A little while later, dressed in a pair of oversized sweatpants I stole from Dash, rolled down at the waist, and a top I hadn't realized had shrunk in the wash, I made my way downstairs. If Leah wasn't already calling "*Mommy*," I would have changed shirts but my munchkin is hungry, and that always takes precedence…unless I want to hear, *I'm starving*, over and over again.

I set all the ingredients on the counter. Leah is mixing the batter, doing her best to slop the mix over the sides, or at least that's the way it looks. I resign myself to a good, long cleaning of the counters.

"That looks finished. Come wash your hands."

Leah bounces over to the sink and stands on the stool that lets her reach the faucet more easily. Once her hands are washed and dried, I grab my mug, and pour myself a cup of coffee. A little caffeine always helps me get the day started.

As I go to take a sip of my coffee, Leah asks, "Did you meet the prince last night, Mommy?"

At the question, I all but spit the liquid out of my mouth. Before I can answer—not that I have a reply, because what can I call Nick—the doorbell rings.

"I've got it!" Leah yells and disappears through the kitchen entryway.

"Leah, do not open that door!" I yell, just as the *beep beep* from the unset alarm signals that my daughter has done just that. The beeps are meant to let me know if anyone enters or exits the house without my knowledge.

I run, skidding to a halt at the open door where Leah stands facing Nick.

"Hi, Mister. You're a stranger. I'm not allowed to talk to you," she says, then shuts the door in his face.

★ ★ ★

Nick

I STARE AT the shut door in shock. A little girl answered. I pull out my phone and check the text from Harrison again, comparing the number on the house to the address on the screen. It matches.

I am still confused as shit when the door opens again, only this time Aurora stands in the entrance. Her cheeks are flushed, and her hair is tousled. After-sex hair, as if a man's fingers spent hours messing up the long strands. My stomach churns at the possibility that there might be a guy inside—a father to that adorable girl, and maybe even a husband to Aurora.

"Nick, what are you doing here?" she asks, her voice strained.

"I asked Harrison to get your address from Xander."

She closes her eyes and shakes her head but doesn't say a word. The little girl has disappeared.

"I thought we could talk," I tell her.

She narrows her gaze, her hand still on the door. "You said you'd call."

"I couldn't wait. And to be honest, I didn't trust you not to blow me off. Not after the way you ran from me last night." I decide to go for honesty, because she looks ready to follow her daughter's lead and slam the door in my face. "I didn't want to lose touch with you again."

"Mommy, you said you'd make pancakes!" The voice who'd called me a stranger shouts, this time much louder.

"Come in," Aurora says, obviously resigned.

What the hell? Is it that bad to see me again?

I follow her inside, and she closes and locks the door behind me. "Leah has a bad habit of answering the door without me being there. I'm trying to break it, but she's strong-willed."

"Like her mother?" I really want to know about the little girl's father but can't figure out how to ask.

Aurora stares at me, a wealth of emotion in her eyes. I have no idea what is going on.

Footsteps stomp towards us and the child stops next to Aurora, tugging on her too-large sweatpants. Men's sweatpants, I think, and my stomach cramps even harder.

Her top, however, is another story. It is short and tight, allowing a strip of skin to show above the drawstring of the pants.

"Mommy, pancakes *please*!"

I get my first real look at her daughter. Blonde hair like Aurora's, a little curlier and more out of control, frames her tiny face. Her features are delicate, and she is adorable. And her eyes—

My breath leaves me in a rush as I take in those indigo orbs so common in every branch of the Dare family.

"How…how old is she?" I manage to ask.

Aurora has gone pale. "She's five," she whispers.

I don't need to do the math. No wonder Harrison asked me how long it had been since that summer in

Miami Beach. My brother works with the Kingstons. No doubt he's met Aurora and her daughter. But without the knowledge that she'd been with me, the color of the little girl's eyes could be chalked up to coincidence. Until my reveal last night.

"Why'd you let the stranger inside, Mommy? Didn't you tell me about stranger danger?" Leah asks.

I bite the inside of my cheek. The kid is a spitfire.

"He's not a stranger, honey. Mommy knows him from when I used to live in Florida." Aurora holds my gaze as she speaks, until I feel the child staring at me, and I drop my eyes to look at her.

"What's your name?" she asks me.

"I'm Nick. What's yours?" I'm surprised I can speak, considering how dry my mouth has become.

"I'm Leah. Do you want pancakes? Mommy, please, you promised and the batter's ready."

I glance over, and Aurora gives me a little nod.

"I'd love to have pancakes," I say to my daughter.

My daughter. Holy shit. I've spent plenty of time regretting the '*no last name agreement*' Aurora and I made that night. We thought it was fun, even smart at the time. But I never wanted to kick my own ass more than I do at this moment.

I follow them through the house—a gorgeous, decorated home that is obviously lived in. What appears to be a box with little girl dresses hanging from the sides sits in one corner of the family room, and a plastic karaoke set-up with a large plastic microphone in the other. I search for signs that a man lives here—not that I know what I'm looking for—and come up empty.

Once in the kitchen, a mess greets me. Pancake batter is dripping over the bowl with a spoon in it and the other ingredients sit on the counter. I feel like I just walked into the Twilight Zone.

"Have a seat and I'll get you some coffee," Aurora says, then goes about taking a mug from a cabinet and pouring me a cup.

In silence, she takes out a frying pan and I space out as she pours the batter into it. While the pancakes sizzle, Aurora expertly cleans the counter, juggles flipping the pancakes, and grabs dishes for their meal.

"Do you have kids, mister?" Leah pulls a chair closer to him and sits down, leaning into his personal space.

She is so damned cute with her outgoing personality and spunk. "I…"

"Leah, let's not be nosey. Nick is an old friend. He and I have a lot of catching up to do later," Aurora says.

And if that isn't an understatement, I don't know what is.

"Do you like butter or syrup on your pancakes?

That's not nosey, right Mommy?"

I laugh and answer before Aurora can reply. "Syrup. How about you?"

"Me, too. I like chocolate chips in mine, but Mommy said no, cuz I had ice cream with Samantha last night." She puts her hands under her chin and lets out an exaggerated sigh of disappointment.

My lips twitch, and I meet Aurora's amused gaze. God, what I've missed out on. I can't be angry at anyone but fate, but damn, it hurts.

Just as Aurora places three plates with pancakes on the table for them, the doorbell rings.

She immediately puts a hand on Leah's shoulder. "Do not move. I've got the door. I'll be right back."

She strides out of the room, and my gaze follows the movement of her hips, her sweet ass in those sweats, and the strip of skin that teases me.

I hear two beeps, then the low hum of conversation. Soon after, Aurora strides back into the kitchen, a man about my age behind her.

"Hi, Mr. Wheeler. Where's Mimi?" Leah asks, her fork in a pancake as she tries to lift it all at once.

The man glances her way. "Mimi is with her mom. I saw a strange car in the driveaway and came by to check on you two."

I narrow his gaze. Is this a boyfriend?

"We're fine," Aurora says. "But thanks anyway."

"Who's this?" The man in the Polo short-sleeved shirt turns his gaze on me. "I assume it's your Porsche out front?"

I rise to my feet. This guy is an ass—I don't owe the man answers. "Who are you?" I ask in return, stepping closer to Aurora. Posturing? Yes. Necessary? Also, yes.

She glances between us, twisting her hands together, her anxiety about the entire situation obvious.

Shit. I don't want to make anything harder for her. I still wondered if the guy with the lean body and preppy look, his brown hair falling over his forehead, is her boyfriend but she isn't acting like that is the kind of relationship she has with this guy.

"Nick Dare," I say, breaking the ice. For her sake, I extend my hand to the other man. "I'm an old friend of Aurora's."

"Mark Wheeler." He shakes my hand.

And I make sure to squeeze. Hard. Because I hate this Mark guy on sight. Hate how his gaze lingers on Aurora's exposed belly. Hate how he assesses me and all but ignores the little girl flopping her pancake on the plate.

"Here." I sit down and cut up Leah's breakfast. "Do you like your syrup all over it or on the side?" Where did that question come from, I wonder.

I'm not used to dealing with kids and know nothing about them. But I want Leah to be happy, I think, as more foreign emotions flood my body.

"All over, Mr. Nick," she says, picking up the plastic bottle and handing it to me.

I do my job, saturating the pancakes as Aurora's voice interrupt my thoughts.

"Mark lives next door," she says. "He has a daughter Leah's age."

Fucking swell.

"Mark, Nick and I were just catching up. Can we talk another time?" Aurora asks.

"I suppose." The man looks from Aurora to me, clearly not happy as she escorts him to the front door.

From what I can deduce, Mark has a hard-on for Aurora, and the feeling isn't returned. In fact, I'm not sure she is even aware of the poor sap's feelings.

Well, if the neighbor thinks he has a chance with Aurora, that notion ends now. I'll make sure of it.

CHAPTER THREE

Aurora

I LET MARK out, refusing to engage in conversation with him about Nick. Our daughters are friends, which is our main connection. And we are next-door neighbors, nothing more. As an ex-cop turned security guard, Mark tends to look out for Leah and me—and I appreciate it. But I have to admit, his behavior today has been odd. Over the top.

With Mark gone, I return to the kitchen to find Leah eating her pancake, which brings me back to the moment Nick ended the men's pissing contest in favor of sitting down and cutting up Leah's pancake so she could eat breakfast. He even asked her how she liked her syrup poured. My entire body heats at the sight of him giving my daughter his full attention.

Our daughter—something I am sure he's already realized.

I step into the room to find Leah engaging Nick in conversation. "My birthday party is soon!"

"When is her birthday?" He glances at me, obviously confused, and I understand why. We met over the summer. I had Leah nine months later.

"April twelfth!" Leah says.

"We had a painting party planned indoors, but Leah came down with a fever and a cold and then croup. She was sick for a week so we had to postpone. Only the place we'd planned to have it was booked every weekend for the next month," I explain.

"So Mommy said if we waited till almost summer, we could have it outside and Ariel could come!" Leah says, barely catching her breath. "Now I want Cinderella because Mommy and I watched the movie and now *she's* my favorite princess. But we already promised Ariel she could come and Mommy said we don't want to hurt her feelings." Leah's explanation involves hand gestures and a lot of rambling.

The twitch of Nick's lips as he tries not to laugh is nothing short of adorable. I thought he was hot last night in his tuxedo. But the guy sitting in my kitchen, wearing dark jeans and navy tee-shirt, is sex on a stick. Muscles I didn't know he possessed bulge in his arms, and the razor stubble on his jaw takes my breath away.

"When is the party?" he asks.

"It's in two weeks on Saturday."

"I also want to invite the prince but Mommy said he's busy." Leah puts her fork down and looks over, giving me a view of her sticky face and hands. I'm about to suggest we wash her up when Leah's eyes light up. "Mommy, can Mr. Nick come to my birthday?"

"Yeah, Mommy. Can Mr. Nick come to her birthday?" Nick parrots, similar eyes to my daughter's sparking with laughter.

"We'll talk," I say to both troublemakers.

It takes another hour for me to get Leah washed up—which includes a bath because her hair is sticky, too—and dressed. Then I call Melly and ask her to take Leah for the day, so Nick and I can talk.

"Bye, Mr. Nick!" Leah calls out as Melly, looking stunned and confused, leads the little girl out the door.

I told the woman who is the closest thing to a mother I'll ever have that I'll explain…soon. Then I called Cassidy and Dash and promised to visit the new parents tomorrow.

All the while, Nick sat in the family room, television on, waiting. At the thought of being alone with him, nerves pulse inside me. And knowing I'll have to explain how I grew up make things even worse.

I finally join him, walking into my favorite room. The overlarge sofa enables me to relax after a long day, something I cherish. I don't have much time to myself these days, and that is also something Nick needs to know.

"Welcome to the madness that's my life," I say pointedly.

He has to understand that life with a child is messy, busy and chaotic. It isn't all sunshine and fun. *Hi, Mr. Nick, come to my party, Mr. Nick.*

He pushes himself to a standing position and gestures for me to come over. "Aurora, you look ready to break. Sit down."

I start for the chair beside the sofa but he lowers himself back down and pats the cushion next to him.

I pause.

"Come on. We need to talk and sitting across from each other like strangers isn't going to make it easier." He treats me to a panty-melting grin, but that isn't what I want from him now. Even if that smile affects me like no man's ever has, before or since.

I settle on the ultra-suede cushion and bend one leg so I can face him. Our gazes meet and hold.

"She's mine," he says.

There is no need to ask—he obviously knows. "She is. I had no way of finding you and—"

He holds up a hand. "Stop. We both know there's no fault here."

"But you came back, and I hid." Which ultimately deprived him of being involved in every stage of his daughter's life so far.

"It's not like you knew you were pregnant and hid it." He reaches out and takes my hand. "Tell me. What could have been so bad that you wouldn't see me again after the night we shared?"

I rub my free hand against the soft sweats, seeking comfort. "I don't know where to begin. My life is—and was—complicated. But I'll start with the things that affect you."

He wraps his fingers around mine. "I'm listening."

Nodding, I blow out a long breath. "The day we met…"

"Your birthday."

I meet his gaze and smile. "You remembered."

His soft gaze meets mine. "I remember everything."

A lump rises in my throat. "That day, I'd aged out of foster care. I know now that there's extended foster care and independent living resources if you meet certain requirements but my case worker rarely showed up. At the time, I had no idea I had options. The family I lived with was only too happy to see me go and the feeling was mutual."

"Jesus, Aurora. I had no idea," he says, his tone low.

That day, I took one look at the table of guys who obviously had money and knew there was no way I could admit my circumstances to Nick.

"I didn't want you to know. The people who owned the diner said I could stay in the back room. It was tiny and hot but I had a roof over my head and they allowed me to take my meals there. As far as I was concerned, I was lucky."

His thumb rubs back and forth over the top of my hand, encouraging me to go on.

I swallow hard. "When you asked me out, it was a bright spot during a really shitty time. We were great together and we connected. But I could tell you were smart, that you came from a good family, and you had money. I had nothing and was embarrassed by that fact. So I decided to make the most of our night together, because I knew it had to be a one-time thing."

A few seconds of silence slip by as he seems to process my story. "And then you realized you were pregnant." He sets his jaw, his tension and frustration obvious.

I nod. "It was scary, but I was determined to make it work. I finished high school with morning sickness. I graduated and began working full-time at the diner. And I found a free clinic where I met a doctor who was kind."

If it hadn't been for that doctor, there was no way that my family could have found me.

"Go on," Nick says.

"The doctor had a girlfriend, and she offered me a place to stay and a real job, working on the books. That meant I was getting a real paycheck, instead of getting paid under the table, the way I had been at the diner. So by the time Linc Kingston came looking for his half-sister, there was a paper trail for him to find."

"Fuck." Nick runs his free hand through his hair, never letting go of me with the other. "How did I miss the fact that you were so alone?"

"I got good at hiding what I didn't want other people to know. But Nick, the doctor who helped me out was Braden Prescott."

His eyes open wide. "My cousin?"

I nod.

Their family story is incredible. One of Nick's uncles, Paul Dare, was the sperm donor for his best friends, the Prescotts, who couldn't have children. The family was sports royalty, all but Braden, the doctor.

"Small world, huh?" I ask.

"Even smaller, me finding you again." His eyes gleam with an emotion I can't name.

Is he really that happy to have found me? How does he feel about discovering he is a father? He's had no time to think about, let alone process, the news. Nor do I know what he intends to do.

I slide my hand from his. "It is. And we have to figure out how to handle things for Leah. That's what matters. That's who is important in all this."

"I agree." He leans in close. "And you need to be aware, I want her to know I'm her father. I want to be part of her life."

I rise to my feet, nerves kicking in. "How?"

"What?"

"How do you want to be part of her life? In what way? Where do you live? What state? Because we're here. My family is here and that's where Leah is staying." I feel myself fraying at the edges as the possibilities spin out in my mind. "What about your life? Do you have a wife? A girlfriend? Are you going to want some kind of custody?" I ask, my voice rising.

Panic fills me as all the possibilities spiral in my mind. No matter what he wants, all I can think about is that I could lose my daughter.

"Whoa." Nick rises and comes up beside me, wrapping an arm around my shoulders.

He smells delicious, like musk and man, and despite everything, my body reacts to his scent, his nearness. But I can't focus on our chemistry. I have to concentrate on my daughter and the life I've built for my child and myself.

He turns me to face him. "I have no intention of trying to take Leah away from you. And there's no wife, no girlfriend, no one but me… And you… And Leah, to worry about."

I force in deep breaths, telling myself to calm down. He isn't the enemy. He is just an unexpected new presence in my life.

"Better?" he asks, staring into my eyes.

"Yes." I still didn't know where he lives but I believe him when he says he isn't going to take my daughter in any kind of custody fight. And that knowledge allows me to relax a little. I've spent the better part of my life alone, relying on no one but myself.

"Good."

"We can't just spring the news that you're her father on her."

He draws in a deep breath. "She can't keep calling me Mr. Nick, either." He laughs, and the tension between us eases.

"Come to her birthday party, spend some time with her and we'll get there, okay?"

He nods. "Okay. But I'd like to see her sooner than that."

He releases his hold on me and I step back, needing space from his heady scent and the effect his nearness has on my body.

I swallow hard. "What if you take that time to process the shock? Make sure you want to be in her life before you come barreling in, only to disappoint her if you disappear on her after the novelty has worn off?"

He visibly clenches his jaw but then nods. "I understand. You need time to adjust, too. But I need you to know she's not a novelty to me."

"Were you always so astute?" I manage a shaky smile. "Maybe I do but I also need to know Leah can count on you. Be sure," I say, aware of the pleading note in my voice.

"I am. But I'll take the time."

I am grateful that he's given in.

"I'm going to get going. I think today has been stressful enough for us both."

"You can say that again." I nod in relief. "Umm, where are you living now?" I ask again.

He braces his hand on the doorknob. "I travel from hotel to hotel around the country, wherever the business needs me. Right now, I don't really have a home base." He shrugs. "But the rest of the family is in New York. Even Harrison moved there from L.A., so I'm here more often than not."

"Living out of a hotel room," I say. A person can't get more transient than that.

How does he expect to have consistency with Leah, if he has a job that has him constantly traveling, and doesn't have a real home? I'm not sure how I feel about that, him drifting in and out of Leah's life. After the childhood I had, I crave stability and am determined to make sure my child has it.

"And where are you staying?" I ask.

"The Meridian Hotel in the city," he says, walking towards the door.

He turns to face me again and without warning, slips one hand around my waist, pulling me flush against him. Every hard inch of his body presses into my softer flesh.

"Wh..what are you doing?" I ask, my voice husky.

His deep blue eyes bore into mine. "What I should have done the moment I saw you again."

I part my lips to speak, but before I can utter a word, he captures my mouth with his. He doesn't linger, but he damn sure makes his point, stroking my tongue with his. Then, too soon, he lifts his head.

"It's good to see you again, Aurora." And before I can say anything, he straightens and lets himself out.

The sound of the door closing leaves me staring after him in shock. My fingers touch the lips he kissed, while awareness ripples through my body. My emotions were all over the place in a quick span of time. One minute I was worried about him taking my daughter away from me, and the next, I was in Nick's embrace. My nipples are hard and panties damp.

God, the man is potent. But I can't do this—not again. If Nick is going to be back in my life, it has to be about Leah. Not us. I won't stand in the way of him getting to know his daughter. But my ability to truly trust someone was shattered a long time ago.

Nick

I AM A father. I am also in shock. I managed to hold myself together at Aurora's, but barely. After all, it isn't every day I discover I have a child I knew nothing about. I went through the motions in a fog, cutting a pancake like a dad and absorbing the fact that the sassy, little chatterbox is mine.

Once Aurora and I were alone, I focused on her. It was easier to concentrate on the woman who still affects me on a sexual and emotional level than to think about the bombshell she just dropped on me. I need time to process that. But when Aurora panicked over my intentions regarding Leah, I realized she was in full on freak-out mode, too.

Knowing the best thing I can do is to talk to someone whose opinion I respect, I drive from Aurora's townhouse to the Manhattan high rise, where my sister Jade lives. I text her, so she knows to expect me. And when I arrive, Spencer, the doorman, lets me up.

I rap my knuckles on the door and my sister answers, greeting me with a hug. "Hey! I'm so glad you're here."

"Hey, yourself." I step back and take her in. Her eyes are glassy and her cheeks flushed—she obviously is still battling a migraine.

"Are you feeling better? It's not like you to skip one of Harrison's premieres."

"It's slowly going away." She shrugs. "I'm used to it but it sucks. Everyone says Harrison was phenomenal."

"He and Sasha had amazing chemistry," I say.

Jade closes the door behind me, and I follow her into the family room. The television is on and her favorite blanket is thrown on the couch.

Picking up the remote, she hits 'mute' on one of the Housewives shows and curls back up on the couch.

I take the other side of the sofa and get comfortable, too. Though I have news, I'm worried about her. "Are you sure this is just a headache?" I ask.

"As opposed to…what?"

"Oh, maybe it's because last night was the date you were supposed to marry Theo Matthews?" Until Zach saw the guy getting too cozy with another woman in a bar.

There was no mistaking their interaction for anything other than what it was. Theo Matthews, hockey goalie, was cheating on Jade. Zach took photos in case Jade didn't want to believe it. Considering he was the second fiancé to fuck her over—the first was in it for the Dare money—I wouldn't blame her for not wanting to face the truth. Jade gave both men the boot, but her heart was shredded in the process.

She frowns. "I'm over the asshole."

"But that doesn't mean you aren't aware of the date. Nobody would fault you for wanting to be alone last night, instead of in a crowd of people." I offered to come over but Jade insisted that I go to Harrison's premiere.

"Can we change the subject? I heard you ran into some woman you met in Miami? Let's talk about that." She raises her eyebrows and stares me down.

I hold up both hands in defeat. "Fine. But if you want to talk, you know where to find me."

Her expression softens. "I do and I love you for caring. I'm okay, really. So, what's going on with you?"

I blow out a breath. "I did run into Aurora last night. And I showed up at her place this morning."

I keep replaying the moment Leah opened the door, and that little face, with *my* eyes, greeted me. A lump rises in my throat. "I'm a father."

"Wait, what? Say that again." She sits upright and stares at me in disbelief.

"Pretty sure you heard me the first time."

She blinks hard. "Shit, Nicky." Only my twin ever calls me that. "Did she keep your kid from you?"

I shake my head. "No. Nothing like that. Aurora and I didn't exchange last names. It was one night and she had no way of finding me once she realized she was pregnant."

Jade's hand covers her open mouth. "Oh God. That poor woman."

I rise and begin to pace the room. "Actually, she was a girl, just eighteen when we met. And it gets worse. She was practically homeless at the time. And I had no idea. Thank God she got a few lucky breaks or who knows what would have happened to her and my kid." My chest hurts at the thought of Aurora living in the back of that diner, in a too warm room, with little money.

"What are you going to do about your…son? Daughter?"

I turn to my sister and grin. "Daughter. Her name is Leah, and she's a spitfire. Not to mention the cutest kid ever."

"Nick, umm, what makes you certain she's yours? That this isn't some elaborate scam for money?" Jade winces as she asks the question.

And I can't blame her for asking it. "For one thing, she has our eye color. And remember those lucky breaks I mentioned she'd gotten?"

Jade nods.

"One of them was going to Braden Prescott's clinic when she was pregnant. Apparently, his now-wife, Willow, took Aurora under her wing and gave her a place to live while she sorted out her life. They also got her a job, which created a paper trail, and enabled the family she didn't know she had, to find her." I pause, letting my story sink in.

When I'm sure Jade is with me, I hit her with the craziest part of Aurora's life. "And...she's a *Kingston*. She doesn't need my money. She's also not the type of woman to scam anyone," I snap, then shake my head. "Sorry. I just know the kid is mine, okay?"

"Okay. You know I had to ask but I get it now." And my sister smiles wide. "I can't wait to meet her. Got a picture?"

I grind my palms into my own eyes. "Dammit! I didn't even think about taking one. Hang on." Pulling out my phone, I text Aurora my request. A few seconds later, a photo shows up on my screen and I grin.

"Here." I hand Jade the picture I intend to make my background photo. Leah, with her curly blonde hair in pigtails and a huge smile on her face, cuddles with a stuffed bear.

"Oh my God, she's adorable! I want to squeeze those cheeks! So what are your plans? When can I meet her? I need to buy her things!" My sister reaches for her laptop, her excitement allowing me to relax now that she isn't questioning my child's paternity.

"Jade, hang on."

"What's wrong?"

"Leah doesn't know I'm her father yet." I run a hand through my hair in frustration. "I showed up at the door, and of course, Aurora introduced me as an old friend. She didn't deny who Leah was to me, but she did ask that we take it slow. Right now, Leah calls me Mr. Nick." I laugh, remembering the first time she said it.

"But she'll let you see your daughter, right?" My sister sounds worried, defensive on my behalf.

"Yes. Leah invited me to her birthday party and Aurora agreed. She said we'd take it from there. I don't want to traumatize her," I tell my sister.

But I have the sense that not much will send my daughter into a tailspin. She seems to be an all-around happy kid, which I owe to Aurora's good parenting. If she wants to take it slow, I trust her judgment. But if anyone is traumatized by my sudden presence in their lives, I know it is Aurora.

"Traumatize who? Aurora or Leah?" Jade asks, causing me to let out a laugh.

"Twinning," I mutter. Despite not being identical—in fact, in looks, we are polar opposites—we often think the same way. "Aurora's more unsettled by all of this than I think Leah will be."

"Speaking of Aurora, what is it you want from her? Just access to your daughter?" Jade rises from her seat. "Can I get you anything to drink? I'm going to get some soda. I need caffeine—it'll help my head."

I nod. "Sure. I'll have a Coke." I follow her into the kitchen, hoping I can avoid her first question since I'm still trying to figure out the answer.

Jade stops at the refrigerator and takes out two cans of soda, handing one to me. "A glass? Ice?"

I shake my head. "I'm fine, thanks." I pop the top and take a long sip.

"You didn't answer me. What do you want from Aurora? What made you show up on her doorstep the morning after running into her? It's not like you knew you had a kid before you knocked on her door, right?" My twin raises an eyebrow, calling me on my bullshit. And letting me in on the fact that she's already drawn her own conclusions.

"Since you've already decided what my intentions are, why don't you tell me?" I take another sip of my drink, letting the bubbles go down my throat.

She smiles at the chance to give her opinion. "What I *think*, is that you like her. *Mr. Three Dates and I'm Out* wants to throw his rulebook out the window." Jade nudges me with her elbow and grins wider. "You think she's gorgeous, you want to kiss her, you want to do her," she sings in the tune from *Miss Congeniality*. Yeah, so I watched the movie with Jade during one of her migraines.

"Quiet, wise ass," I mutter to my sister. "Yes, I

want to get to know Aurora now and see what could happen between us. And yes, I wanted that before I knew we could be…a family." I almost choke on the word. And for good reason.

After all, I have four siblings. My biological mother, who had mental issues, ran off when Jade and I were only two years old. I don't like to think about what she did next. Our father then married the nanny, and Serenity had raised my siblings and me as if we were her own. I even call her mom as she is the only mother I've ever known. She also has four kids with my father, triplets from fertility treatments, and an oops baby afterwards. After being surrounded by so many kids for most of my life, I crave solitude and the idea of settling down, getting married, and having children of my own has never really occurred to me.

Jade is silent, obviously contemplating everything I told her. She lets out a long breath. "Aurora has been through so much. I'm glad she ended up with a good family who has her back. But that doesn't mean she doesn't have issues from growing up in foster care and being abandoned by the people who were supposed to take care of her."

"What are you saying?" I ask.

"Just that you're used to women falling at your feet. I don't see that happening with Aurora."

I raise an eyebrow, wondering if I should be insulted.

Before I can decide, my sister continues. "I'm also saying, the Dare charm might not be the answer to getting what you want, in this case. You shouldn't have any problem building a relationship with your daughter but maybe, you should temper your expectations with her mother."

I dip my head and put my can on the counter. This isn't the advice I want to hear.

She places a hand on my shoulder. "On the positive side, being a Dare has its benefits. We're a persistent bunch. And you, more than the rest of us, know how to get what you want." She rises and presses her lips to my cheek. "You got this, little bro."

I roll my eyes at the familiar sentiment. "Just because you were born ten minutes before me, that doesn't make me your little brother."

She laughs. "Do you want to hang out for a while? We can talk some more…or not. Whatever you want."

I nod, grateful for the support. "Maybe you can help me figure out what to pick up as a birthday gift for a little girl who doesn't even know I'm her father."

We throw our soda cans into the recycling bin and return to the family room to watch some television. And for me, it's the chance to do some soul searching as well.

★　★　★

Aurora

I SIT ON the closed toilet seat, watching as my daughter plays in the tub.

"Mommy, would you read me *Cinderella* for my bedtime story?" Leah asks, letting me soap up her hair with shampoo.

That choice will mean more questions about the prince, I think wryly. "Sure, honey."

"Who's Mr. Nick?" Leah asks, playing with the cup I normally use to rinse the soap from Leah's hair.

Nick. I expected Leah to have questions about the man who had breakfast with us. I'm actually surprised it has taken this long.

"I told you this morning. He's someone I knew when I lived in Florida. Tip your head back so I can rinse the shampoo."

Leah tips her neck and head and scrunches her eyes closed. "I like Mr. Nick."

"That's good, because you're going to be seeing him more often," I murmur. And someday soon, I am going to have to tell my daughter that Nick is her father.

I fill the cup and pour the water over Leah's soapy hair, careful to keep one hand on her forehead, blocking the soap from getting in her eyes. I repeat the action a couple of times before adding conditioner to the ends of Leah's hair, then rinse that out, too. "Okay, you're good. Head up, eyes open."

Leah blinks hard a few times and rubs her eyes. "Is Mr. Nick coming to my birthday party?" she asks, not deterred from the subject on her mind.

"We'll see." Although Nick told me he'll be there, I don't know him well enough to set my daughter up for disappointment in case he doesn't show up.

I pull the plug, letting the bathtub drain, then rise to my feet and pick up the towel, holding it up. "Careful getting out." I help Leah with one hand and then wrap her up in the big towel.

"Brr. It's cold!"

"Mommy's got you." I rub the towel over Leah's arms and legs and wring out her hair with another towel.

"Mommy, Grandma Melly asked me what I wanted for my birthday!"

I smile at the mention of the grandmother I never thought my child would have. "Oh yeah? What did you tell her?"

"I want a pony!"

I briefly close my eyes and pray for the strength to raise this child. "No pony."

I will have to make sure Melly knows that. With the money the Kingston family has, a pony just might seem like a reasonable request.

"Come on, honey. I forgot your pajamas. Let's go into your room and get dressed. I'll get the hair dryer ready."

As Leah runs out, my thoughts turn to Melly Kingston. What an amazing woman she turned out to be. When I had first arrived in New York with Linc, pregnant and feeling very alone, Melly gave me a place to stay. She treated me like a daughter and became Leah's grandmother. Not once has she treated us badly because I am her deceased husband's illegitimate child.

I did go from rags to riches, much like the Cinderella story Leah so loves. But my life hasn't been anything like a fairytale. It left me emotionally battered and scarred. My real mother, Tiffany Michaels, got pregnant accidentally. Like mother, like daughter, I think, shaking my head. The difference is, Tiffany hated being a parent and turned over custody of her child—me—to her mother, my grandmother, when I was five. One year later, my grandma suddenly passed away and I was sent to foster care.

Once Linc found me, I discovered there was more to my story, and it was even worse than anything I ever conjured up in my imagination. I hate to think about my early life—the abandonment, the neglect— because it only serves to remind me of how unwanted I actually was. By both parents.

Shaking, as I always do whenever I think about

what my so-called parents did to me, I push them out of my mind. I force myself to remember that my new siblings and their mother are different. They welcomed me. Accepted me. They aren't anything like Kenneth Kingston or Tiffany Michaels. And that is why I legally changed my last name to Kingston. I am part of a family now. Blowing out a deep breath, I will the shaking to stop just in time for Leah's return.

Dressed in her pajamas, Leah walks into the bathroom and drops her damp towels on the floor. All I have to do is look at my daughter, and love wells up inside me. I would do anything for my little girl, to make sure she has the most amazing life possible. She will always know she is loved—something I myself so desperately needed.

Just because I now have money, I have no intention of spoiling Leah. I'll teach her values and help her understand the need to give back.

"If I can't have a pony, I want a puppy!" Leah exclaims.

I sigh and bite back a grin because there is no way I can handle adding a dog to the chaos that is our lives. Still, I know I am kidding myself if I think Leah won't be over-indulged by her aunts, uncles, and now her father.

Oh, God. Nick. He really is a part of my life now. I alternate between thinking I can handle it…then I break out in a full-blown panic attack.

I pick up the towels and hang them on the hooks behind the door. "Nothing that's alive for your birthday present. We don't have time for a puppy right now. You're in kindergarten and Mommy's busy with her charity."

"Fine," Leah says with an exaggerated sigh and drop of her shoulders.

"Come on. Let's dry your hair so we can read *Cinderella*." I pick up the hair dryer I plugged in.

"The part about the prince!"

By the time I finish with Leah's hair, then tuck her in, read her the requested part of the story, where Cinderella slips her foot into the glass slipper and lives happily ever after with the prince, give her two sips of water because Leah is *so thirsty*, and she finally falls asleep, I fling myself onto my bed, exhausted.

I must doze off because the ringing of my phone startles me awake and I reach over to see Nick is Facetiming me.

Drawing a deep breath, I sit up and take the call.

CHAPTER FOUR

Nick

A FTER I LEAVE my sister's, I drive to the hotel where I am staying. The Meridian NYC is a part of the group of hotels my siblings and I bought from Robert Dare, an ostracized family member. We saved the business from bankruptcy and added to their holdings. I am responsible for checking out the hotels, travelling often, and putting out fires where necessary, while Jade is based in New York, where she takes on the role of lead Event Coordinator. She oversees events and budgeting for all the hotels, but she is hands on at the Meridian NYC.

I head to a suite I co-opted for my visit and settle onto the bed, pulling out my phone. I don't know what time Leah goes to bed, but I give calling both my girls a shot. My stomach twists in unfamiliar knots at the thought. Neither of them is my girl. Leah won't be mine until she knows she can call me 'daddy'. And Aurora? Hell if I know what she is to me. But I need to find out.

Calling her is a start, and Facetime will let me see

them both.

When Aurora answers, it is obvious she's been asleep. Her hair falls across one cheek, and the other shows a sleep line on her fair skin. Though I feel bad for waking her, I can't deny the intimacy inherent in seeing her with her guard down, almost as if we've woken up together in bed. My dick hardens at the thought, something I'll have to take care of on my own. Though I'll use my own hand, it will be Aurora I envision gripping my cock and the sudden desire to reach through the screen and touch her is almost overwhelming.

"Nick?" She shifts positions and sits up, resting her back against the headboard and pillows.

"Hi." I clear my throat. "Is this a bad time?"

She shakes her head, pushing several long strands away from her face. "No. It's okay. I dozed off after Leah's long bath and bedtime routine."

"Tell me more." I want to hear everything about my daughter.

Aurora laughs, the melodic sound not helping the desire for her already pulsing inside me. "She's something else." Her eyes light up as she describes Leah's antics and I find myself laughing along with her.

Aurora grins at me and our gazes lock and hold. My breath catches and my heart pounds hard in my chest. Something passes between us, reminding us of the day I first laid eyes on her. It had been an indefinable connection—something I can't put a name to—but I never felt it with anyone else. It was a deep yearning that pulses between us.

"Are you coming to Leah's party? It's in just over two weeks." She breaks the silence first. "I know she put you on the spot and you might have plans."

I raise my eyebrows. Does she really think I would miss it? "Even if I had something on my calendar, I'd reschedule. Don't worry. I'll be there. Which reminds me… what can I get her for a gift?" I don't know anything about five-year-old girls and though I can ask my mother… Shit. I haven't told my father and Serenity they have a grandchild yet.

I need to call them before the family text chain handles it for me. If they heard already, they'd have called me by now.

"Well, Leah told her grandmother that she wants a pony." Aurora's eyeroll tells me what she thinks about that idea. "When I said no, she requested a puppy. I nixed that idea immediately, too." She tucks a strand of hair behind her ear and swipes her tongue over her lips.

I do my best not to groan, wishing it was me tasting that sensual mouth.

"I told her we were too busy to deal with any living being at the moment." Aurora's lips quirk in a smile.

"As for you, anything from a toy store in her age bracket will work."

"I want it to be something special." I don't know when Aurora will agree to tell Leah about my place in her life, but in the meantime, I intend to make an impression.

"Hmm. Well, she wants an outdoor playhouse. There are quite a few brands and some can run a lot of money. But you don't need to spend a fortune. They make adorable plastic ones. She just wants a place to play with her friends in the backyard. She'd be thrilled if you picked out one of those."

"I can do that," I say, my excitement palpable, now that I have something concrete in mind. "Okay, so we've talked about Leah. What about us?"

Her eyes open wide. "What about us?" she asks in a husky voice.

"I want to take you out on a date." The words hang between us, along with all the years that have passed.

"Nick, I don't know…"

"I want to learn more about Leah. Her favorite foods, maybe see some baby pictures. All the things I missed." Yeah, I am not above using my daughter to get what I want when the truth is, I need to know. "And I want to learn the same things about you." A hole settles in my chest and only Aurora and knowledge about my little girl can fill it.

"You make it impossible to say no to you," she says, that mouth I want to kiss pursed in thought.

I grin. "That's the point. I'm going to come up with something we can do that will let us talk and do something fun. And don't worry. I'll give you plenty of time to get a babysitter."

"You're trouble, Nick Dare."

I wink at her pretty face. "I've only just begun to turn on the charm."

Although my sister warned me it won't work on Aurora, I know of no other way to reach her other than to be myself. "Get some rest and we'll talk tomorrow."

She opens her mouth to reply but I wave and hit end before she can come up with an argument. I am ahead and intend to stay there.

I call my father and ask if he and Serenity can come into the city for lunch tomorrow. I have something important to tell them.

Aurora

THE NEXT MORNING, I take Leah next door to play with Mimi. Mark opens the door and smiles at the sight of me. Wearing a pair of khaki shorts and his typical collared short-sleeved shirt, hair combed and slicked back, he looks like he's been waiting for me to arrive.

"Well, if it isn't my two favorite ladies," he says, stepping back so we can come inside.

I'm not comfortable. Until yesterday, Mark was a good neighbor who's always come across like a platonic friend. A single dad, we often help each other out with babysitting, play dates, and the like. His sudden interest feels awkward for me.

"I'm sorry, but my sister is coming over. I need to get home. What time should I pick up Leah?" I ask.

He frowns, disappointment evident on his face. "I was hoping we could share lunch."

"I'm sorry. I'm in a rush." I bend down to talk to Leah. "Are you excited to play with Mimi?"

Leah nods. "I have my Barbies!" She holds up the case she stuffed her dolls and their clothes into.

"Okay, I'll see you in a few hours." I kiss her cheek and rise to my feet.

Mark steps aside. "Mimi is in her room. You can go find her."

Leah runs inside and I take a step back. "Thanks, Mark. I'll text you when I'm on my way back to get her."

Before he can attempt to coax me inside, I turn

and walk back home.

Chloe arrives a few minutes later and we drive to a local restaurant for lunch. A little while later, we are sitting at a window seat, drinking mimosas and waiting for our lunches.

"Okay, girl, spill it," Chloe says. "I've waited long enough for you to bring up the subject of Nick Dare on your own. I already know he's Leah's father. What I don't know is the whole story. Even Mom doesn't know everything." Chloe points to her glass. "So drink up and explain."

I take a long sip and fill Chloe in on yesterday's events. "All he had to do was take one look at her and he knew," I say. When I realized he figured out that Leah was his, my heart nearly stopped.

"What happens now?" Chloe asks as the waiter places our meals on the table.

"He wants to go out on a date. To get to know me again." Oh, I know he used wanting details about his daughter as an excuse to get me to agree. The man is smooth and isn't above using my daughter against me.

"Are you going to go?" Chloe picks up the ketchup, then pours some on her plate so she can dip her French fries.

"We are…"

Chloe narrows her gaze. "But? I can hear the hesitation in your voice."

Ignoring my hamburger, which means I *have* to be upset about something, I glance at my sister. "Do you have any idea how long it's been since I went out on a date?" My stomach twists at the thought.

Chloe picks up a fry and dips it into the ketchup. "Umm…I guess I hadn't given it any thought. I know you've been busy with Leah and your charity but—"

"Nick," I say, interrupting Chloe. "That night with Nick was the last time I had sex," I blurt out.

I went out on a date—once—since Nick. The guy and I went back to his place and made out, but when he realized I had a kid—courtesy of a babysitter's phone call with a question—he couldn't get rid of me fast enough.

And my first time? That was with some guy from high school in the backseat of his car. I wasn't even one hundred percent sure he'd gotten all the way inside me before he came. *Eew.* Why am I thinking about that now?

Chloe drops her French fry back on the plate. "Oh jeez."

"Right. And now I'm supposed to go out with the father of my child, who has made it pretty damned clear he's interested in me." I sigh. "I've been on my own my entire life. It was hard enough to let you guys in. How in the world can I trust Nick?" I finish off my mimosa and let out a long breath. "Did I mention he doesn't even have a home? Forget a house, but not even an apartment. He travels from city to city and stays in family hotels."

Chloe winces. "That's hard." She signals for the server and the woman walks over. "Can I help you?" she asks.

"Two more mimosas, please." Chloe asks.

"Of course." The server walks away.

"Another drink will help," Chloe says, glancing at me. "Now you're going to listen to me. I understand your fear. Remember how Beck and I met? Dumped bride, remember? But sometimes the scariest things turn out to be the best things that ever happen to you. We can agree that it'll be good for Leah to have her dad in her life, right?"

"Yes? But what do we know about Nick? The man is basically a transient. Realistically, how can he be in her life in a way she can count on? And he's a chick magnet." A hot, sexy man I want to climb like a tree. But that won't happen because Nick and I need to co-parent and I have a plan for my life that does not include a man.

I need stability and can now provide it for my daughter and myself. I am an independent woman and don't need anyone coming in and out of our lives at a whim. I know I have an unhealthy fear of abandonment, but eighteen years of anxiety can't be undone overnight.

"Sounds to me like you're making excuses. Get to know him better, and then decide if you want him in your life as anything more than Leah's father. And for heaven's sake, clean out the cobwebs!"

"*Eew!*" I cry out, then lower my voice. "*Eew.* My battery-operated boyfriend works just fine," I say quietly. "And he stays in his drawer where he belongs and does not come with a list of demands. He's very reliable."

Chloe raises her eyebrow. "He doesn't hold you at night, either. I'm just saying, try to be more openminded. And eat. Your burger is getting cold."

"Fine." I pick up my food and take a bite, slowly chewing, savoring the taste.

I think about Chloe and the point she's trying to make. Yes, I miss the feeling of having a man's arms around me, the scent of masculine cologne—Nick's in particular. I also like the appraising way he looks at me, those gorgeous eyes darkening when he thinks I'm not paying attention. I feel the same quickening when I glance at him.

But it was one thing to have sex with a man I can blow off the next day, and another to get involved with the father of my child. What if things between us don't work out? Leah will be the one to suffer. And I can't let that happen.

I have to admit that I am looking out for myself,

too. I was hurt enough as a child. Neglected, unwanted, ignored and thrown out on the street as soon as I came of age. If I let him in, Nick will be in my life forever. But I can't deny him access to his child.

I take a deep breath, decision made. I'll go out with him and tell him all about his daughter, and anything else he wants to know.

But I'll be sure to keep my distance.

That way, nobody will get hurt.

★　★　★

Aurora

AFTER DROPPING LEAH off at school on Monday, my next stop is the boutique baby store in town. After all, I can't walk into Dash and Cassidy's place empty-handed. I am sure baby Freddie won't want for anything, so I pick out a few of my favorite items, things I often used when Leah was born.

By that point, my fortunes had changed. I lived with Melly, and the woman overwhelmed me with the amount of baby things she bought. Six weeks before, I was terrified I wouldn't be able to afford diapers and baby clothes. But that all changed when Linc found me. Melly put a nursery together in her home, giving me my own wing with Leah. My eyes fill at the wonderful memories and the gratitude that is always with me. I will never forget where I come from, nor will I ever take the life I have now for granted.

I drive the hour and a half to East Hampton and pull into the driveaway of Dash's house. Leaving all the gift bags in the car, I stride up the front walk.

No sooner do I ring the bell than Dash flings open the door. "I'm a father!"

I laugh at his greeting. "Yes, you are. More importantly, how's the new mom and baby?" I ask, stepping past him and walking inside.

"They're both perfect," he says in a soft voice I rarely hear from my rock star brother.

"Congratulations," I murmur and pull him into a hug.

He steps back, a huge grin still on his face. I am so glad he's gotten a second chance with Cassidy.

"Cass is in the nursery, rocking the baby. You can go on in," he says.

"I came bearing gifts, so you can unload the car." I pat him on the cheek, hand him my keys, and rush to the nursery. I already saw the room. I was there as they worked on getting it ready.

I step into the doorway. The new mom sits in a gliding rocking chair, humming as she holds her baby in her arms and pats him on the back.

I tap lightly to let Cassidy know I'm there. "There's

nothing better in the world, is there?"

Cassidy glances up and gives me a tired smile. "I didn't know I had so much love in me."

Nodding in total understanding, I walk into the room decorated in soft, neutral pastels.

"Want to hold him?" Cassidy asks.

"You know I do. Let me wash up." I step into the attached bathroom, soap up my hands, rinse and dry off. Then I return and gently scoop the tiny baby from his mom's arms.

I move the blanket that bundles Freddie so I can get a better look at his tiny face. "Oh, he's so sweet." Leaning down, I kiss his forehead, inhaling his baby scent.

Cassidy rises to her feet, wincing as she moves.

I remember the pain well, too. "If you want to go shower, take a nap, hang with Dash, or just eat something, I can stay for a couple of hours. I don't mind giving you a break."

Cassidy sighs. "I'd love a shower. Dash was going to take over for me, but knowing you're here…"

"I get it. There's a steep learning curve and no manual." I glance at Freddie and smile. "I'll just sit in the chair and enjoy him."

"You can put him in the bassinet in our bedroom if you get tired. Thank you," Cassidy says. She walks to the door and turns. "I may be overwhelmed with all things baby, but I heard you have news—Nick Dare was the one who had you running away at the premiere?"

"I didn't run…not exactly. I was in shock. I'm sure Chloe filled you in, right?" I ask.

Cassidy nods. "The major points."

"Nick is Leah's father?" Dash asks, joining us. "Do I need to kick some Dare ass?"

I straighten my shoulders. "No!" Obviously, Chloe hasn't told them everything. "I didn't know his last name when we… It wasn't his fault. I had no way of finding him once I realized I was pregnant." I draw a deep breath. "And now you know everything."

"Except whether or not he's going to step up." Dash reaches for his son.

I hand the infant over and smile at my big, bad, rock star brother holding the tiny baby. Then I meet his gaze and turn serious. "Nick and I are handling things. There's no need for you to get involved."

"If you need back up, you call me," Dash orders.

As much as I want to argue with his tone, I know it comes from a good place—one of caring. "I can handle him. But thank you anyway." I kiss his cheek. "Now give me back that baby so I can cuddle him. You go spend some time with your wife."

Dash nods. "Let me change him and he's all yours."

And that tells me all I need to know about how hands-on this daddy rock star will be.

Aurora

THE REST OF the week isn't as much fun as the baby visit was. I wonder if I'll survive long enough to host Leah's party. My daughter is so excited, it's hard for me to get anything done. Every night, Leah bounces around as if she's eaten a plateful of pure sugar and putting her to bed each night isn't easy.

Thanks to kindergarten and it being Mark's day for pick up, I am able to go to the office. My charity, Future Fast Track, FFT for short, provides housing for kids like myself who have nowhere to go. Even now, Linc is looking into finding a building, and I am trying to figure out how we can manage it.

But my charity provides a lot more than just a place to stay. It also offers skills training, education and support, with the goal of helping these kids become self-sufficient adults. The charity also aids them in making connections, to help them in avenues of employment or education.

Since I can't help every foster child in the country, I started in Nassau County where I live. The main requirement to qualify was that the young person has to remain in the foster care system until his/her eighteenth birthday. Then, along with my partners—Sasha, Cassidy and the assistant I hired, Billie Coale, once a foster child herself—I work to get them help.

Today has been a good day, and I arrive home, planning to grab a snack before I pick up Leah from Mark's.

But instead of being able to grab a few minutes of peace and something to eat, I come home to chaos. An unfamiliar landscape truck is parked out front, and I walk around back to see what is going on. Three men are constructing a white wooden playhouse with a pink door—an impressive looking full-size playhouse that has to have cost a fortune.

I shake my head and glance around, immediately catching sight of Nick. Wearing a pair of jeans, a gray t-shirt with muscles bulging from the sleeves, his face covered with scruff, and sunglasses over his eyes, he looks scrumptious and very, very kissable.

He also has an overly satisfied expression on his face that wipes out my desire and replaces the feeling with fury.

"She's going to love it, right?" He gestures to the house in progress. "It has a fake kitchen with a sink, stovetop, and utensils. There's a doorbell that rings. And the sign with her name on it will be ready by the time of her party."

The sound of hammers echoes throughout the yard. My neighbors probably want to throttle me. Oh God. Has Leah seen this from next door? "Are you kidding me?" I ask him, now riled up enough to let him have it. Did he even *hear* what I told him?

"Excuse me." A man I didn't noticed walks over to Nick. "I'm the electrician. The guys said to speak to you about porch lights?" The guy points to the play-house, which has mini light fixtures on either side of the front door.

A squeak escapes my throat, and Nick has the good grace to wince before facing the man. "Tom is the contractor," Nick says. "He's the guy in the baseball hat. He'll work with you on whatever you need."

"Thanks." The man strides across the lawn to find Tom.

I glare at Nick. "Inside, now." Without waiting, I spin and walk around front so I can let myself in.

He follows and once I turn off the alarm, I put my purse down on the couch in the family room. I try counting to ten and back, but it doesn't make a dent in my fury.

Doing my best to remain calm, I turn to face him, finding him way too close. It's difficult to really let into him when all I want to do is grab him and kiss him senseless.

"Nick, I said to buy her a plastic playhouse, not an actual house that needed construction!"

He nods. "I get that. I do. But every little girl would love a place like that to play in."

I open my mouth to argue but he holds up a hand and I let him continue.

"Soon enough, Leah is going to find out I'm her father. I'd like her to know I didn't just bring any old present but something special." He looks at me with pleading eyes.

I sigh, understanding his need to make up for lost time but this isn't the way to go about it. "You've seen Leah. She's an easygoing kid. She already likes you, *Mr. Nick*." I can't help the grin lifting my lips.

He laughs. "You're right. I'm just nervous I'm going to screw things up, so I figured a grand gesture would hide my flaws."

Dammit. Just when I work up a healthy, well-deserved dose of anger, he has to open himself up and let his vulnerability show. I sigh. "You don't need a grand gesture, and you definitely don't need to buy her love. She's going to be thrilled just to have a father."

That is definitely true. Kindergarten has been fairly easy on me. Mark helps me out now and then, and there are other children at school with different kind of families. There have been one or two awkward events where I asked one of my brothers to step in—the daddy/daughter picnic for one—but overall, I've managed.

"You're saying I went overboard. But since the playhouse is already up…" Nick says in a tone that all but begs me to let the house stay.

"Yes, Nick. You went overboard." I burst out laughing, mainly to keep from crying.

Just as I thought, Nick Dare is going to be impossible to control.

★   ★   ★

Nick

I FIGURED GIVING Leah a real playhouse might be risky. But hell, I had to pay through the nose to have it delivered and installed in a ridiculously short period of time. Still, it's worth it. It isn't every day I get to make a first impression on my daughter.

Or my daughter's mother.

The sight of Aurora, in her black slacks that narrow to sexy high heels and a beige camisole that outlines her full breasts, hit me harder than I could believe. I fell for the young girl in jeans and a tee-shirt, and am equally attracted to the woman in the designer clothes.

I step closer, the heat of her body calling to me. "I can't believe we have a daughter."

Her eyes grow damp. "I know. I'd have told you if I'd known how to find you."

I nod. I'm not angry at her. "I wish I'd been there for you through it all."

She manages a smile. "Well, you're here now, so I guess we'll have to make the most of it."

Reaching out, I tuck a strand of hair behind her ear, and she shivers at my touch. "Does that mean the playhouse stays?" I ask.

Her light laughter causes warmth to settle in my chest.

"Yes, the playhouse can stay."

"I appreciate it. And I'll make sure I come to the party early to help you out." Leah might not know I'm her father yet, but I am, and it's time for me to step up.

Her surprised gaze meets mine. "That's sweet, but I hired a company to bring tables and chairs. They'll take care of setting up. But I'm sure I'll be able to put you to good use."

Unfortunately, I'm leaving tomorrow for a pre-planned trip to L.A. to surprise the manager there who has been dropping the ball lately, so I won't be around to offer that much help. I'm not sure how to tell Aurora about my plans but I figure she'll understand I need to work. And I intend to be at her place early, the day of the party.

"How many people are you having that you need that kind of set-up?" I ask.

She laughs and I love the sound. "Are you forgetting how big my family is?"

"Right. Crazily enough, mine's even bigger."

Those words hang between us in a way I didn't plan.

"Nick, I'm sorry. I'm sure you want them here, but we need to go slow. For Leah's sake."

"I get it." I nod, agreeing with her as much as I hate the fact that it will be another year before my family can celebrate my daughter's birthday.

"Thank you." Her gaze meets mine.

We stand within kissing distance, her head tipped towards me, and the urge to close the gap and fasten my lips over hers is strong. One wrong move could tip the scales. I could bring her closer or scare her away.

While an internal war wages inside my mind, my body knows what it wants. Instinct has always served me well, so I slide my hand behind her neck, pull her close and seal my mouth over hers. Her lips are soft and part immediately, allowing me to slip my tongue inside. Pleasure and desire mix, consuming me, and confirming this woman belongs with me. And now, I just have to prove it to her.

I rub my tongue against hers and a low moan escapes her throat. The sound goes straight to my cock, but doing anything about *that* would be acting too soon. If I take advantage of our desire now, she'll have plenty of second thoughts later.

"Mommy! Is that playhouse for me!"

Aurora jumps out of my arms just as Leah comes bounding in through the front door.

"Hey, honey! What are you doing here? I thought you were with Mimi." Her cheeks flushed, Aurora takes another step away from me.

"She saw all the commotion outside and insisted on coming home to find out what was going on." Mark, the douche neighbor, walks in behind Leah. A little girl with long brown hair, who I assume is his daughter, skips in beside him.

"Mr. Nick!" Leah yells.

"I think asking her to use her inside voice is pointless at the moment," Aurora says to me, her eyes lighting up at the sight of our daughter.

I grin at the bouncing ball of energy. "Hi, Leah."

"Is the house mine, Mommy?" She stares up at Aurora with hopeful eyes.

Aurora looks to me and nods. "It's a birthday gift from Nick, honey. What do you say?"

"Thank you!" she yells.

Aurora rolls her eyes. "Okay, now that the surprise

is over, how about you lower your voice, okay?"

"Okay, Mommy. Can me and Mimi go play in it?" she asks much more quietly.

I shake my head, visions of her getting hurt on the pieces of wood and scattered nails flashing through my mind. "You need to wait until the men finish putting it together. Right now, it's not safe to play in."

I feel Mark's heavy stare. Shoving my hands into my pockets, I stand and glare back.

"Girls, why don't you go play in Leah's room?" Aurora suggests, obviously not missing the tension in the room.

The two kids run out, leaving the three adults alone.

"That's some gift," Mark says, glancing between Aurora and me.

I narrow my gaze, assessing the man. Aurora said Mark is nothing but a neighbor, but his jealousy is obvious. I set my jaw, determined not to piss off Aurora by getting into it with the other man.

"Yes, it is." Though '*It's a present for my daughter, asshole*,' is what I really want to say.

"Especially from an *old friend*," Mark says.

I narrow my gaze. "Your point?" I want nothing more than to inform this *neighbor* that I am Leah's father, but it's Aurora's decision who to tell and when.

Aurora steps forward, putting herself between the

two of us. "Whatever this male bullshit is…" She gestures between us. "Let's not do it with the girls in the other room."

God, her take-charge attitude turns me on, but I can't help being glad that her anger isn't aimed my way.

She steps back and glances at Mark. "I don't think Nick's gift is anyone's business but his."

The other man's cheeks burn with embarrassment. "I just meant…" He shakes his head. "Never mind."

"Thank you for picking up Leah and keeping her at your house this afternoon," she says, her voice taking on a sweeter tone that has me grinding my teeth. "Mimi is welcome to stay for dinner."

Mark shakes his head. "I promised her we'd go out for pizza. I'll go grab her and we'll get going." He stalks off in the direction the girls went.

Knowing when to shut my mouth, I remain silent until Mark and his daughter leave and Aurora has shut the door behind them.

Since it's quiet, I assume Leah is still in her room and use the time to corner Aurora. "I didn't mean for things to get awkward."

She sighs. "I've never seen Mark act like that before."

"Has he ever had male competition before?"

She sucks in an audible breath. "That's not…not

what you are…or what he is," she says, wringing her hands and obviously flustered.

"Oh, I beg to differ." The man wants Aurora, and he lives next door. And that makes what I'm about to tell her even harder. But I know better than to push her. Early days, I remind myself.

She shakes her head. "It's too quiet. I should check on Leah," she says, changing the subject.

"One second. I need to tell you something first."

She raises her brows. "What is it?"

I shove my hands into my front pockets. "I'm going to be away for a few days on business, but I'll be back in plenty of time to help you get ready for Leah's party."

Upon hearing the news, she freezes, her body stiff before shaking off whatever is bothering her. "Oh. Okay. Good to know." She steps back. "Like I said, I need to check on Leah. Can I let you out so I can lock up first?"

"Yeah, sure." I'm uneasy as she leads me to the door. Before she can grab the handle, I turn to her. "Aurora, I *am* coming back."

"So you said."

"But you don't believe me?" Her sudden stiff demeanor tells me my leaving has hit a nerve. I know she's had a tough life but obviously I need to learn more so I could understand her triggers better.

She steps away from my touch, and I feel the loss. She is nothing like the woman who just melted in my arms.

"I believe you," she says. "And I understand that you have to work. All I ask is that you don't make promises to Leah that you can't keep."

If I didn't already have a good idea of how deep her distrust runs, I would be insulted. "I wouldn't do that." But her history obviously taught her differently.

If I am going to reach her, I need to find out more about her past. Was it foster care that made her so wary or something more? I need to get her to confide in me, to trust me. And once she does, I hope I'll manage to break down the walls she keeps so high.

She steps aside and opens the door. "Have a safe trip."

I brush my knuckles over her cheek, ignoring the sheen coating her eyes. Oh yeah, I definitely brought up some deep-seated issues. "I'll be calling. Facetiming and texting you, too."

She treats me to a brittle smile. "I'll let Leah know."

"It's not all about Leah," I say in a serious tone. "Have a good week. You'll be hearing from me." Knowing she needs space, I open the door and force myself to walk out.

CHAPTER FIVE

Aurora

N ICK'S *FEW DAYS* away turn into almost two weeks. The time drags by, and though I hate to admit it, I miss him. With the time difference, as well as the long meetings he's been in, and dinners he's had to attend, it's been hard for us to touch base very often, or have any kind of meaningful conversation when we do. I take it as a sign—this is how things will be if I ever try to have a real relationship with him.

As for Leah, Nick calls during dinner so he can talk to her every day. Although he makes the effort for Leah, I feel like an afterthought. I ought to be used to feeling this way—I've endured enough broken promises in my life. And really, all that matters is that he is there for his daughter. Every little girl deserves for her parents to care. I might have been young, but I vividly remember my mother dropping me off at my grandmother's house—for good. My mother promised to visit, but she never did.

When my grandmother died and my mother never reappeared, I put aside any fantasies I held of ever seeing my mother again. Every foster parent assured me I'd have a place to stay, but too often that wasn't the case. Either the kids already living in the house didn't want me there and picked fights so the frustrated parents gave up and asked to have me re-homed, or I was sent away for some other bullshit reason.

My daughter deserves more than someone who will be in and out of her life, calling himself daddy. Though phone calls are a poor substitute for Nick's presence, at least he keeps his promises to our daughter. As for me, it's better I see now how things with Nick will be, before I let my heart get involved. Leah's party is in a few days, and I hope Nick shows up as promised.

On the Thursday before the party, I walk into FFT's office and find Billie at her desk, pouring over spreadsheets.

"Good morning!" I stop and drop my bag onto a nearby chair. "How goes it?" I ask the pretty girl with pink hair and black framed glasses.

Billie slides her chair back and smiles. "Pretty good! You know how we discussed the fact that so many of the kids who we're able to get jobs end up being fired due to lack of experience or whatever other situation they're dealing with?"

I nod, lowering myself into the other chair. "It's definitely been an issue."

"Well, as you suggested, I did some research. There's a charity in Texas who had the same issues. So they decided to open a café—one that hired kids who were still in the system, allowing them to train ahead of time."

"I remember seeing something about that café on a news show." I lean forward in my seat. "Tell me more about it."

Billie glances at the computer and scrolls down the screen. "*La La Land Café* has an eight-week internship where the kids learn life skills. They're mentored, so they have someone to support them, and they're taught customer service, as well as other on-the-job training. The only issue is that not everyone wants to work in the service industry." Billie glances at me. "So they created an outreach program to encourage other businesses to do the same thing. This gives the kids a better chance of succeeding in the real world." Billie's light blue eyes gleam with excitement.

I mull over the explanation and how it can apply to what FFT already has in place. "You're suggesting we set up something similar, find businesses where skills can be learned *before* the kids get into the world after foster care."

Billie points a pen at me and grins. "Bingo."

"So we'd have to reach out to schools in order to find applicable kids."

Billie nods. "That's what I've been doing. Creating a list of schools, contacts, and businesses in each area."

"That's great. Brilliant idea, Billie!" I'm so lucky that Billie answered my employment ad two years ago. The young woman is currently twenty-two years old and has a smart, go-getter personality. She is a huge asset to FFT, and I knew it. "I'll run it by the board and see if there are any employers we currently work with, who might want to participate."

Billie beams at my acceptance of her idea. My board consists of Sasha, Cassidy, myself and a couple of benefactors my brother Linc vouched for when I had created my charity.

Leaving Billie to her research, I go into my office and make some business calls. Several hours pass, and I am getting ready to leave so I can stop home before I pick up Leah, when Facetime rings on my phone.

I glance at the corresponding screen on my laptop, shocked to see Nick's name. I immediately accept the call, and his face appears.

"Hey, gorgeous."

My body warms at the name. "Hi, yourself." I intended to be cool to him and treat him as casually as he's treated me, but one glance at his handsome, clean-shaven face and I know there is more going on than I realize.

He looks tired. The whites of his eyes are bloodshot, and the crinkle lines around them are more pronounced. Despite feeling forgotten earlier, I can't help but worry about him now. It makes it hard to keep an emotional distance when I want to reach through the screen and rub the frown lines away.

"Where are you?" he asks. "I don't recognize the background.

I glance behind my desk at the large water color I chose for the wall. "In my office at Future Fast Track. It's the charity I run." We never talk much about the parts of my day-to-day life that don't involve Leah.

"Tell me about your work there," he urges.

I shake my head, knowing now isn't the time. "Nick, you look exhausted. Is everything okay out there?"

He groans. "I'm having some staffing issues. I had to fire the manager and I've been working around the clock to put things in order. I'm still not sure whether I want to hire from within the company or bring in someone from the outside."

"I'm sorry to hear that," I murmur.

He shrugs and runs his hand through his thick hair. "I'm much more interested in your life than the shit going on here. I already know Leah's doing well. I talk to her every night. Tell me about the work you do with your charity."

Since that is an easy question and something I'm passionate about, I dive into the answer, explaining the reason I created FFT, what its purpose is and Billie's new angle. Nick asks questions, I answer them, and before I know it, I've been talking for almost half an hour about my job. I trail off, suddenly embarrassed.

"Wow. That was a lot. I'm sorry. I'm sure you simply asked to be polite. I tend to get carried away when it comes to this subject," I say, feeling the heat in my cheeks.

His gaze bores into mine. "I think you're pretty damned amazing, giving back the way you do."

His admiration makes me feel good. "It's so rare for someone like me to ever be in this position, going from rags to riches. I need to give back."

He nods in understanding. "You told me Linc came to Florida. How did he find out about you?"

I still. I can't believe how much I've already confided in him, but something about the distance between us makes it easier for me to open up. But talking about this? It's beyond humiliating, something I've hidden in my mind. I'm not sure I can admit it out loud.

He leans forward, as if to see me better, and I focus my gaze on his lips, which only serves to remind me the man knows how to kiss. God, I am so conflicted about him. Not about our attraction but about my ability to trust anyone after what was done to me.

"Aurora, come on. Talk to me."

I close my eyes and sigh. "Okay."

★ ★ ★

Nick

I'VE HAD IT with this extended trip. How the shit going on in this hotel has gone unreported is beyond me. I thought I'd simply fly in to fire the manager, expecting the assistant manager to step up and take over, or at least buy me time to hire someone more qualified. Only it turns out the lack of good leadership at the managerial level has trickled down to all aspects of the hotel. I've spent hours meeting with employees in all of the departments, and I'm exhausted.

Although I've made time to speak to Leah every night while she has dinner, I know in my gut I've been neglecting speaking to Aurora alone. I want to call her each night, but my family business keeps me busy. Dirty Dare Vodka, though Asher's baby, is something each sibling looks after. Investors need wining and dining, and since I'm in town, Asher asked me to handle it.

I have a free hour now, and I call her, hoping we can catch up. I didn't expect things to turn so personal. Maybe some distance is what we need for her to feel comfortable enough to talk to me. And if that means I made headway with the emotional walls she's erected, I'll take it.

I've been sitting in a chair in my hotel room, but now I move to the bed to get more comfortable, propping my iPad on my lap and settling in to listen.

Looking gorgeous for work, her long blonde hair hangs over one shoulder in a long braid and she has a full face of makeup, though I like her just as much, if not more, without any. Hell, I just plain like her, though I suspect the feelings floating inside me are already something more than that.

"How did Linc find out about me?" She repeats my question, and I remain silent, not wanting to say anything that might make her clam up. "When Kenneth Kingston...I can't bring myself to call him my father, died of a heart attack, Linc was the one who'd looked after his estate. I guess the man was old school, at least in his dealings with my mother." Her mouth twists at the word. "Linc found eighteen years' worth of canceled checks written to Tiffany Michaels."

"Your mother," I say, because it's obvious.

Aurora nods. "Linc hired a private investigator, who tracked her down." She shifts in her seat and draws a deep breath. "My whole life, I thought she was dead." She looks me straight in the face. "Why else wouldn't she have come for me after my grandmother died?"

My chest squeezes tight. The pain in her voice, and her expression, guts me. I'm furious at myself for asking her about this when I can't comfort her in person. I need to hold her in my arms and soothe her pain, not have a screen and the entire country between us.

"I'm sorry, baby."

She closes her eyes and damned if a tear doesn't leak from one eye. She grabs a tissue from the side of her desk and dabs at it, her cheeks flushed with what I sense is embarrassment. Dammit.

"Do you want to stop talking about this?" I ask in a gruff voice. "I never should have pushed you."

She shakes her head. "I'd rather get it over with."

I nod, but my jaw is clenched so hard, I think for sure I'll crack my teeth. "I'm here."

I force out the words, feeling inadequate. But I've started this conversation, and her pain is worse than mine.

She sniffs and twirls her braid around her hand. "I guess it's obvious at this point. My mother accepted monthly child support checks, cashed them, and used them to live her best life."

I run a hand over my face. "She admitted this?"

Aurora nods. "She didn't want to be saddled with a

child. Apparently, Kenneth wanted her to get an abortion. But she refused because she knew he'd pay her to keep silent. He didn't want his wife finding out about me."

I blow out a harsh breath. "What about after your grandmother died? I'm sure the state tried to contact one of them?"

Her eyes fill again and she dabs at the corners with the already damp tissue. "My mother didn't want me. She refused to take me and signed off on all parental rights. And I guess part of the financial agreement between Kenneth and my mother was that he not be named on the birth certificate. So, to all appearances, since I had no parents, I went into foster care."

"Fuck."

"The story gets uglier, so buckle up," she mutters.

"I'm listening," I say in as comforting a voice as possible.

Aurora draws a deep breath before speaking. "A year or so before he died, Kenneth paid my mother a visit, informing her he wouldn't pay her another dime after I turned eighteen. God knows why he even cared at this point. I mean he'd already been shelling out money for so long and he could afford to do it forever."

I wait for her to gather her thoughts and continue.

Eventually, she shrugs her shoulders. "When Kenneth found my mother, he discovered she hadn't been raising me at all. So I'm sure that made him feel even more justified in cutting off her funds immediately. After all, why wait for my birthday?"

My jaw hurts from how hard I've been clenching it. "I assume your mother didn't take that well?"

"No." Aurora picks up a pen and begins rolling it between her palms, as if to calm herself down.

Once again, my need to touch and comfort her is almost overwhelming, but there is nothing I can do.

"According to Linc, Kenneth had been suffering from early dementia and had begun making erratic, secret deals, things Linc couldn't understand when he discovered them after Kenneth's death. So maybe deciding to visit my mother had just been one of those impulses. Or maybe he just wanted to exert some control over her. But he failed. My mother threatened to tell his wife about me."

My stomach churns even more. "Something tells me your mother wasn't his only mistress. Tiffany would be opening a huge can of worms for your father if she told his wife."

Aurora nods, curling her hands around that pen. I know something bad is coming. "I was *seventeen* when Kenneth went to see her," she says softly.

I close my eyes as the threads of the story come together. "You were still in the system." Anger like

I've never felt before fill my veins. That mother fucking son of a bitch had left his daughter in foster care.

I don't care if it was just one year more. Anyone with a shred of humanity would have rescued their child and given her a home.

"Neither of my parents wanted me." Her soft voice carves a hole in my chest. "Do you have any idea what it would have meant to me if he'd taken me home when he found out my mother wasn't raising me? I'd still have been angry he hadn't wanted me all those years before, but at least I'd have known someone cared enough to pull me out of that awful foster care system."

I want to throw my iPad across the room, do something that would make me feel less impotent. But this isn't about me.

"Aurora?"

She refocuses her wet gaze on mine.

"Thank you for telling me."

She nods. "I wanted you to know why I'm so adamant about Leah being raised by parents who not only love her, but who she can count on."

A smile pulls at my mouth. Leave it to her to make this about our daughter. But I also understand why. Shifting the focus allows Aurora to think about something other than the pain of being unwanted and unloved. It also lets her keep those walls high. She can't bring herself to trust me because she fears I'll hurt or abandon her the way the two people who were supposed to protect her did. And I still don't know what foster care was actually like for her. Something tells me I won't enjoy that story any better than I liked this one.

She clears her throat. "So that's how Linc found me," she says, as if she can end the story and move on, emotional barriers in place.

I know better. Armed with knowledge, I know what I'm up against. "Baby, I need you to hear me."

She meets my gaze. Though she looks more vulnerable than I've ever seen her, she is even more beautiful to me.

"You're strong and brave and you've had to rely on yourself for far too long." Linc may have swooped in and made her life better, but inside, she is still that unwanted little girl. "It's going to take a while for you to realize it, but I'm in your life for good."

A genuine smile lights her face. "I know you're going to be a good father and I believe you when you say Leah can count on you. I know you'll do your best."

Once again, she is making it all about Leah. And I get it. She figures I'll do my best, which in her mind isn't good enough, because she is talking to me through a tablet screen. I'm not there, in New York, with the woman and child I want to make my family. Sure, there are parents who travel for work, but those people have been in their child's life from the beginning. Aurora's life experience has skewed her view of just about every aspect of life.

I need to wrap things up in California or pull in someone else to handle the hiring.

I want to be *home* with my girls.

★ ★ ★

Aurora

MY TALK WITH Nick leaves me shaken and feeling as though I've opened a vein and bled out in front of him. But I don't have time to dwell on it. I have to focus on Leah. And before I know it, Saturday has arrived, and Nick is at my door, showing up an hour before Leah's party.

I welcome him, and he brushes a kiss on my cheek, his touch leaving me tingling. Then I lead him to the cluttered kitchen, where party favors sit in a basket on the counter, and bowls of food fill the table.

After catching my breath, I turn to face him. In his jeans and collared Polo shirt, he looks mouth-wateringly sexy. He is still clean shaven, and I can't decide if I prefer this look or a little less tidy, with the scruff I imagine scraping my skin as he kisses his way down my stomach… my sex pulses, and I shiver, realizing just where my thoughts have gone.

Shit! How could I let my mind wander like that? Obviously shredding my soul hasn't stopped me from wanting him.

"Are you okay? You're flushed." Nick reaches out and brushes his hand over my warm cheek.

"Fine." I mentally shake myself. My goal is to co-parent, not ogle him. "I'm fine."

He eyes me warily then nods. "Good. Okay then, why don't you put me to work?"

"There's really not much to do. You can help me bring out the chips and M&M's bowls, and put them on the tables outside, to start with." I point to the purple and turquoise snack bowls—their colors matching the Ariel-themed party.

"Where's Leah?" Nick asks.

"I left her watching *The Little Mermaid*. I'm trying to stall putting on her dress until right before the party. She's been begging to use her playhouse for the last two weeks but I wanted to save it for today. I'm lucky she's mesmerized by the movie or I wouldn't have been able to get ready this morning."

I'd be lying if I said I didn't have Nick in mind when picking out the tight olive green, glossy leggings I wear, with a matching sleeveless tank that flares at the waist with cutouts on one shoulder. The casual outfit is perfect for an outdoor party, and if I get cold, I have a matching jacket.

But Nick's arrival has caught me by surprise, and I'm dressed only in the tank top and leggings. He looks so hot, my body reacts and I feel my nipples harden with need. I turn away and get busy sorting the food, hoping he won't notice.

He strides up behind me, and I feel his warmth at my back. "What are you serving from the food truck out front?" he asks, his breath warm in my ear.

I shiver at his nearness. "Pizza and pasta for the kids. A couple of other choices for the adults. The kids are pretty young, so most of the parents will be staying."

He brushes my hair off my neck, and his lips linger on my skin. My body, already prickling with awareness, lights up even more, and despite my best efforts, a low moan of pleasure escapes my throat.

"Nick, this isn't a good idea." But I can't bring myself to move away. He smells so good. A musky scent teases my senses and tempts me to turn around and bury my face in his neck, breathing it in deep.

"Relax," he says in a gruff voice. "I just want to be close to you."

Dammit. How can that come out so sweet when my entire body is on fire?

"How did your family take the news about me?" he asks. "Am I going to be dealing with barely-veiled brotherly threats all day?" His hands slide onto my hips.

"Probably." I let out a laugh. "But Dash and Cassidy are home with their newborn."

"No worries. I came prepared to ease their concerns." He reaches around me and picks an M&M from a bowl.

The act causes him to lean against me and the hard length of his erection settles against my back. I swallow hard. "How did your family take the news about Leah?" I ask.

"I told Jade, my twin, in person. And the others heard pretty quickly through the family grapevine. Everyone can't wait to meet her." He lifts his hand. "Open your mouth."

I obey, which pisses me off, and he pops the small chocolate candy onto my tongue. I move it around and begin to chew. "God, I love these," I say as the chocolate melts in my mouth.

"I know. I bought you a packet from a small store on the beach, remember?"

A lump settles in my throat. "I do." It was after we had dinner and before we went to his hotel. "We took off our shoes and walked along the water's edge as I ate them."

He had held my hand, and I had asked him questions about college. Knowing I would never be able to experience it for myself, I was curious about what life was like without burdens and worries. I knew, even then, that we had no future.

"Mommy! Can I put my party dress on yet?" Leah comes bounding into the kitchen at her usual speed and volume. She stops at the sight of him. "Mr. Nick!"

"I think the mister has to go," he says, chuckling into my ear.

I grin at that. I draw a deep breath and turn to my daughter. "I'll come help you get dressed, and Nick can carry the bowls outside. And Leah, you can just call him Nick. Mr. Nick isn't necessary."

I meet his gaze and see the longing in his expression. He wants to tell Leah who he is to her. I know it and understand.

Maybe after the party today. I touch his hand. "Soon, okay? I promise."

He nods, his expression softening before he turns to our daughter. "Hi, Leah. Are you excited for your big day?"

Her eyes light up. "I'm so excited!" she shouts.

"Let's go get you dressed. Nick, the door leads right out to the backyard. Can you put one of each bowl on every table? Thanks!" Taking Leah's hand, I walk to my room where I keep the dress to protect it from grabby hands.

As I walk with my daughter, I allow myself to relax a little, grateful for some breathing room away from all that is Nick.

★ ★ ★

Nick

AURORA INTRODUCES ME to her family before taking off to greet the girls who are arriving with their parents. Even though I joked about her brothers giving me shit, I know what to expect and am prepared. After all, if some guy knocked up Jade and showed up six years later—even if he didn't know of the baby's existence—I would be pissed.

I spend the day being grilled by sibling after sibling; Xander, the former Marine and current bestselling author and screenwriter, Chloe, the other sister in the Kingston family, and most politely, by Melly Kingston, Aurora's surrogate mother. Chloe and her husband, Beck, have a two-year-old daughter, Whitney, who clings to her father's legs, while Jordan and Linc's son, Jasper, who is almost six, joins the kids. Leah seems to look up to her cousin and follows him around, causing me to grin.

Meanwhile, I patiently answer their questions, all

of them leading up to what my intentions are when it comes to both Leah and Aurora. I tell them my relationship with Aurora is between us, but as for Leah? Well, I plan to be in my daughter's life. They all seem satisfied with my answers, but I know they are watching me. I can feel their gazes on the back of my neck.

As I meet Aurora's family, I keep an eye on my daughter, watching her run around with her friends and enjoy the playhouse I had built. The structure takes up a massive amount of space, and something about making my mark on the place where Aurora and our daughter live pleases me.

Though I want to catch Aurora and talk, she is busy making the rounds between the parents she obviously knows, checking on the kids, and making sure there is enough food and drink. That doesn't stop Mark from sniffing after her all day, though, pissing me off and keeping me on edge.

Especially since I have the distinct feeling Aurora is avoiding *me*. I have no doubt our short time together before Leah walked into the kitchen threw her. Hell, I knew we still have chemistry, but even I was shocked at the way I felt when I was with her. The sensation is unlike anything I've ever felt before, with any of the other women in my life. And after the emotional reveal of her past, I can't blame her if she is shoring up her defenses.

I'll let her try. But I intend, slowly but surely, to break down each one.

Leah, wearing a purple and teal princess dress, runs towards me, and before she can rush by, I snagged her under her arms and swing her up so she sits in my arms.

"Having fun, princess?"

She smiles wide. "Today is the best! I love my house."

"I'm glad. What did you eat for lunch?" I ask.

"Pizza!"

"Did you save room for cake?"

She nods. "Hi, Uncle Linc!" Leah cries out, waving excitedly.

"Hey, pretty girl." Aurora's brother reaches out and tugs on her long curls.

Linc is the only one who hasn't yet confronted me, and I know the oldest brother will be the most difficult. After all, he was the one to find his sister in the first place. It makes sense that he is the most protective of them all.

"Leah, do you want to go back to your friends so Uncle Linc and I can talk?" I ask.

Linc raises an eyebrow. Obviously, he didn't expect me to man up and deal with him directly.

"Okay, but will you be here when Ariel comes?"

she asks.

I laugh. Little does Leah know that I arranged for Ariel to have a 'plus one'. "I wouldn't miss it." I set her down on her feet, and she races off again.

I turn to Linc. "Let's have it," I say, ready for this final inquisition to be over with.

"She's a great kid," Linc says, arms folded across his chest.

I nod. "I agree. I can't wait to get to know her better."

Linc, obviously the master of long silences, studies me. "My sister's done a great job raising her alone," he says at last.

His wife, Jordan, a pretty woman with long, dark hair, walks over in time to hear his comment. "Really, Linc?" She grabs his arm and snuggles into his side. "You're going to try and intimidate the man who couldn't possibly have known about Leah?"

I grin. I like Jordan already.

"Not the point," Linc says through gritted teeth. "He's got a reputation, just like his brothers. And from what I've heard Harrison say, this one's motto is three dates and he's out."

Fucking swell. Harrison didn't realize joking about my dating history would come back to haunt me one day.

"I'll tell you the same thing I told my brothers, *and*

the women I've asked out. I think it's better to be honest, up front, than drag something out when I know it won't work. That said…you're talking about my past." I glance at Aurora, who is smiling at something Leah said. "She's my future."

I didn't plan on admitting that to anyone in her family, but I have a feeling that if I don't stake my claim, Linc will make my life damned hard. And I already have my hands full dealing with Aurora's insecurities. I don't need her big brother interfering.

Linc eyes me warily but nods, as if he accepts the pronouncement. Not that his disapproval would stop me at all, but my pursuit will be easier if Linc doesn't interfere. "Goes without saying, you hurt them, you answer to me."

Jordan grins and rolls her eyes, patting her husband's shoulder.

"If I hurt them, I'll slit my own wrists," I mutter.

"I like you," Jordan says.

I grin. "Gotta say, I like you, too."

"That's enough." Linc pulls his wife tighter against him.

Still smiling, I glance across the lawn in time to see Aurora at the gated edge of the property, talking to a Disney princess. "I take it that's Ariel and Prince What's His Name?" I ask.

"Prince Eric," Jordan laughs. "You need to learn

your princesses, daddy."

She might be amused, but I take my role seriously. "Damn, I have a lot to learn."

"I thought Aurora said she'd only arranged for Ariel to come today." Jordan tips her head to the side, watching the couple enter the yard.

I shrug. "I might have asked Harrison to talk to Cassidy and find out which company Aurora called. Leah's got a thing for princes, too."

"It's Ariel and Prince Eric!" As if on cue, Leah shrieks and runs across the lawn, a group of girls following behind her.

"Interesting." Linc assesses me some more. Then, without warning, he slaps me on the back, and taking Jordan's hand, he walks away.

I start across the lawn, wanting to catch up with Aurora. I only hope she has a weakness for princes, too.

CHAPTER SIX

Aurora

T HE DAY WAS a success, I think. Prince Eric and Ariel joined everyone to sing happy birthday to Leah, who made a wish and blew out the candles. Although I had no time to talk to Nick, I thanked him for his contribution to the party. Of course, he made sure his newfound daughter had her prince. It seems we are going to have to have a talk about not spoiling Leah, but I still smile at the thoughtful gesture.

After what seems like hours, but in reality, is only another sixty minutes, the cake is eaten, the Disney characters go home, and all the guests depart—all except Mark and Nick. I don't expected Nick to leave, and Mark normally helps me clean up after a party. But given Nick's presence, I'm surprised he stayed.

I do my best to ignore the twisting in my stomach about having to deal with both men. Then, we all clean up in silence, dumping the plates and utensils into a big green garbage bag. The party company that delivered the tables and chairs will be picking them up tomorrow, and I don't have to be home for their arrival.

Leah and Mimi are inside watching cartoons on television, and I won't be surprised if Leah is already passed out and fast asleep.

"You did a great job with the party," Nick says, coming up beside me.

Does he have to smell so good? I can't very well not breathe around him, but inhaling his potent scent arouses so many feelings, it's hard for me to sort through them all.

"Not a bad effort for someone who never had a birthday party of her own, huh?" I try to change the subject, but slip and let my vulnerability escape. Again.

Nick puts a hand on my shoulder and squeezes tight.

"You know I'm here, too, right?" Mark asks, joining us from outside, a tied garbage bag in his hand.

Nick opens his mouth to speak but I put a hand up. "Nick, please take the garbage and toss it into the pail in the garage. Mark, let's go talk."

I lead my neighbor to the hallway where we can speak without being overhead. "Mark, what is going on?"

"I should be asking you that very question." A hurt look crosses his face.

I sigh, knowing I have to nip whatever *this* is in the bud. "Nick is Leah's father," I say softly. "She doesn't know yet." I don't feel as if I owe him any more details.

"Wow." He blinks, obviously stunned. "That explains a lot. So, he's here to get to know his daughter?"

I briefly close my eyes, then open them again. God spare me from dense but well-meaning men. "Nick and I have history and unfinished business." I'm not sure if the latter is true but it is kinder than telling Mark I'm not interested in him.

"I thought if I gave you time, you'd come around. We're good together," he says, stepping closer.

I move back. "As friends. I'm sorry, Mark."

"Are you and he…?" He trails off and I straightened my shoulders.

"That's none of your business." I fold my arms across my chest, suddenly uncomfortable. "You should take Mimi home. It's been a long day."

He nods, and after another lingering look, he walks towards the family room. A few minutes later, he's collected his daughter and her gift bag. I let them out, leaning against the door once he is gone.

Once I regain my composure, I check on Leah, who has indeed fallen asleep on the sofa while the television plays in the background.

"Well, that was awkward and unexpected," I say as I reentered the kitchen and notice the counters are clean. Nick has done a good job finishing up while I was dealing with Mark.

Nick leans against the granite counter and studies

me. "Are you seriously telling me you had no idea he has a thing for you?"

I'm not even tempted to tell him off for asking or inform him my private life is none of his business. That unfinished business I mentioned to Mark is alive and well.

I understand Nick's disbelief about Mark because I feel the same way. "I kid you not..." I shake my head. "Until you showed up in our lives, he was my friendly next-door neighbor and we had kids in common. But according to Mark, he was giving me time to come around."

Nick narrows his gaze. "Could that have happened?" he asks, stalking closer.

This is my easy out. *Tell him yes*, a voice in her head insists. If I'm interested in someone else, he'll have to back off and turn his focus to his daughter.

"Aurora?" I move, and he backs me against the refrigerator, invading my personal space. "Are you at all into your neighbor?" he asks in a dark voice, that heaven help me, turns me on.

"No. But that doesn't mean you and I can get involved." No matter how much my body wants him.

He raises an eyebrow as if to contradict me, but I have the perfect excuse to back up my statement. "There's a little girl in the other room who can't have her parents screwing around and messing up any chance at co-parenting in peace." My heart slams rapidly against my chest, my words belying what I really want.

"No matter what happens between us, Leah is my priority, just as much as she is yours."

He speaks with such conviction, I believe him. "Then you agree we should keep our relationship platonic."

I am proud that I am able to suggest such a thing when my body throbs with need for this man. But I don't want to rely on him only to be disappointed in the end. I am still finding it difficult to believe that the Kingstons welcomed me so easily into the family, and that the tight bonds of love between them are now mine, too.

Nick reaches out, sliding his fingers through my hair. "We have a second chance, Aurora, and I don't intend to squander it. That is, unless you tell me you don't want me to kiss you," he says, his forehead touching mine. "Then I'll back off."

Arrogant, frustrating man. He probably sees my hard nipples beneath my snug shirt and notices my body trembling with desire.

"I'm not looking for a relationship," I say. I close my eyes. Why don't I just tell him to back off, that I don't want him to kiss me? I swipe my tongue over my dry lips, and he groans, low and deep.

My eyes fly open, and his deep blue gaze locks on mine. "Say it, and we'll be nothing more than those platonic co-parents you mentioned."

Though I know he's too cocky, and his confidence in getting past my emotional walls should be another reason for me to be careful...

"I can't," I whisper, as his lips come down on mine.

I've been wanting this all day. Every time I caught sight of him across the lawn, saw him with Leah, noticed him watching *me*... I wanted him. But things are just so damned complicated between us, and I am too afraid to let him in.

But that doesn't stop me from reacting to his kiss. And when his tongue sweeps over my lips, I open and it doesn't seem that complex at all. I taste a hint of chocolate and know he's been eating candy. I want to eat him.

So I do what my body craves, push all thoughts out of my mind, and let myself feel. I wrap my arms around his neck, keeping him close, inhaling his scent. Need washes over me, and I rub my body against his, letting arousal settle inside me.

He nips at my lower lip, then licks with his tongue, and I can't get enough. Not because it has been so long since I've been kissed *like this*, but because Nick was the last one to devour me, and now I know—

nothing about the way we reacted to each other was a fluke.

And that makes my life so much more frightening.

As if he is in tune to my feelings, he slows down and backs off, ending the kiss but not moving away.

"I'm not going anywhere," he says. "Not when my family is here."

I know he isn't referring to his siblings, and my stomach flips. *Family.* It is something I never had and desperately want to give my daughter. But do I dare? I have no doubt Nick will be in Leah's life. Whether or not he *stays* or remains part of mine is another story.

His phone rings in his pocket at the same time Leah walks into the room, barefoot, her hair wild and tangled. "Mommy, can we open presents now?"

Nick holds up a finger and steps out of the way to take the call.

I deliberately chose not to have Leah open the gifts at the party for a number of reasons. I didn't want to make the day all about *things,* or make any of Leah's guests feel bad if their parents aren't as well-off.

"It's really not a good time," Nick says to whoever he is talking to. "I'm not joking. I'll call you later, and we'll discuss it." He disconnects the call, a frustrated look on his handsome face.

"Is everything okay?" I ask.

He nods. "We can talk about it later."

Nerves take up residence in my belly but I nod.

"We're going to open presents! Are you going to stay?" Leah asks.

Nick bends down to her level. "Do you want me to?"

Leah nods, her enthusiasm so real, because that is all children know how to do—be open and honest and true. And that makes what I am about to do so much easier.

"Then I'll stick around," he says.

"Yay!"

I smile, and Nick rises to his feet.

"Leah, your first present is a big one, and it's something Nick and I want to tell you about together."

"What is it? What is it?" Leah jumps up and down, causing both Nick and me to laugh.

I glance at him.

Obviously surprised, I see the question in his eyes, and I nod, slipping my hand in his and squeezing it for support.

I look from Leah to my child's father. "Let's go into the family room so we can sit and talk."

★   ★   ★

Nick

MY HEART POUNDS hard in my chest as we settle onto the sofa, side by side. The presents from the party are a distraction across the room, but Leah doesn't seem to notice, as her gaze darts from her mom to me. She obviously senses something huge is about to happen. I push the business call I took a few minutes ago out of my mind. I'll deal with the California hotel issues later. Nothing is more important than this moment.

"So, remember when you had Muffins with Mom Day and Donuts with Dad at school?" Aurora asks. She glances at me. "I let the principal have it for doing things that aren't inclusive, but that's for another time," she says with a laugh. "There was nothing wrong with Bagel Breakfast and bring a friend," she mutters.

I can imagine her, pissed off on her daughter's behalf.

Leah blinks. She is so damned cute, with her wild hair and pink frosting stains around her mouth. "Yeah, I 'member."

"What did you ask me that day?" Aurora strokes Leah's hair. "God, you need that nest brushed." She leans over and kisses Leah's cheek. "Do you remember?" she prods.

"I asked why I didn't have a daddy." Her voice lacks its normal sparkle, and she curls her legs beneath her.

A lump rises in my throat. I hate that I missed out on those important things. Worse, she's been hurt, because she obviously knew something is different about her family.

"And what did Mommy tell you?"

Leah stares at Aurora with the most serious expression I've seen on her face yet. "That all families are different."

Aurora nods. "Yep. What else?"

"You said that even though I didn't have a daddy, I had aunts and uncles who loved me." She rubs her eyes but doesn't look away from Aurora, whose gaze darts to me, then back to our daughter.

"And?"

"And even though we couldn't find my daddy, he loved me very much," Leah says.

Holy shit. She covered my ass even when she didn't have to. Now I am near tears.

"Right. So, what if I told you I *found* your daddy?"

Leah's eyes open wide. "You did!?" This time, she has her loud voice, and I know she's excited. "Where is he?" She looks all around, her big eyes landing on me.

Out of the corner of my eye, I see Aurora nod at me.

I am up.

Drawing a deep breath, I look at the little girl who captured my heart the first time I laid eyes on her. How do I do this? What do I say?

"Leah…" My voice cracks, and I can't bring myself to be embarrassed. I clear my throat. "Leah, I'm your daddy."

She blinks. "Why couldn't we find you?"

Leave it to my kid to be smart about it.

She's stumped me. How do I answer in a way she'll understand and accept? "It's a long story. But I'm here now, and I want to do all the things I missed. Like Daddy Donut Day." I look to Aurora for help, but she's smiling…and leaving me to fend for myself. "Would you like that?"

Leah climbs to her knees and looks me over. "You're really my daddy?"

I nod.

Next thing I know, she jumps into my lap and wraps her little arms around my neck. "I missed you, Daddy."

Jesus. Has anything ever felt so good? I hug her back and glance over her shoulder. Aurora watches us, tears in her eyes.

Before either of us can speak, Leah releases me.

"Can I open presents now?"

Oh, to be a child, and let things flow in and out so easily, I think.

"Bring me a pen and paper so I can make a list of who gave you what. You'll need to write thank-you notes," Aurora says.

Leah has already run for the kitchen.

"Check the junk drawer and go potty before you come back in!" Aurora turns to me. "You did well," she assures me.

"I've never felt so much pressure in my life. Not to mention, she's a sassy little thing. Like her mom." I grin, and Aurora laughs aloud.

"Listen, before she comes back, I have a question for you. I know I said I'd give you plenty of time to get a sitter, but is there any chance you can get someone for tomorrow night?"

I want time alone with her.

Hands on time.

She bites down on her lower lip. "I can manage that. Leah wants a sleepover at her grandma's anyway."

And that reminds me—I need to talk to her about setting up a time for our daughter to meet my family. But right now, I have my work cut out for me. I intend to give Aurora a night she'll never forget…just before I break the news that I have another business trip coming up that I can't put off.

Aurora

I MUST HAVE lost my mind. Why else would I agree to join Nick on a scenic helicopter tour of Manhattan right before sunset? We take a limousine from my house to Westchester County Airport, where we are given a safety briefing before boarding for the private tour for two.

Nick told me to dress comfortably and casually, so I wear a pair of dark jeans, a light blue tank and a white jean jacket in case it's cool—something I end up grateful for once we take off.

I'm shocked when we pull into the airport and even more surprised at what he's planned. Waiting for me inside the aircraft is a bottle of champagne and two small cups along with a bouquet of white roses. We wear headsets, which allow us to talk and hear the pilot narrating as he flies.

I expected an upscale restaurant and intimate conversation, which I prepared for all day. To say I'm blown away is an understatement. The man has gone all out to give me a special night.

Nick reaches over and takes my hand. He remains silent as we look out the windows at the gorgeous orange and yellow view of New York City highlights.

We take in Central Park and Yankee Stadium, along with the Empire State and Chrysler Buildings. I'm floored by the view of the Manhattan skyline and squeeze Nick's hand the entire time he's pointing things out, feeling closer to him than ever before.

When the helicopter portion of the night is over, I grasp my flowers, he picks up the champagne we haven't yet opened, and walk back to the limousine.

Once we climb into the back, the driver shuts the door behind us. Although I have misgivings about getting romantically involved with Nick, everything about the evening has set me up to simply relax and enjoy it. Since I rarely take any time for myself, I push my worries to the back of my mind for the night. Tomorrow will be here soon enough.

"Have fun?" he asks.

I nod. "It was spectacular," I murmur. "I'm still fairly new to New York and haven't seen all the sights yet. But to see them just as the sun set..." I sigh. "I'm grateful for the experience. Thank you for it, as well as the flowers and champagne."

He chuckles. "The champagne came with the tour. It was billed as a romantic flight. The flowers were all me, and you're welcome. They remind me of you. They're gorgeous."

He winks, and my stomach flutters as it only does for him.

"You're a charmer." Suddenly exhausted, I rest my head on his shoulder and close my eyes.

"We have an hour ride back to the city, so you have time for a nap, if you want."

I lift my head up in surprise. "We're not going back to my house?"

He shakes his head. "No. Now put your head back down and rest. I have more planned for you. And you're going to need your strength."

Dear God, his words and actions are a potent combination.

He pats his shoulder, indicating I should do as he asks. When I comply, he wraps his arm around me and holds me close. I doze off, my senses overwhelmed by Nick's masculine scent and his strong embrace.

I'm not sure how long I slept, but I wake to find the car coming to a stop, and Nick saying my name.

I lift my head and stretch the kink in my neck. "Where are we?"

"My hotel. But it's not what you think." Nick's grin sends butterflies bouncing in my stomach.

The driver opens the door and lets us out.

Curious, I let Nick take my hand and lead me into the building. He greets the doorman, then walks through the beautiful marble lobby to the elevator. A few minutes later, we are in his suite.

Inside, we kick off our shoes, and he leads me to a

small dining area where a table is set up. Candles are lit, and a man wearing a white professional chef's coat walks out of what I assume is a kitchen. Another man in a suit steps up behind him.

Nick keeps a hand on my back. "Aurora Kingston, I'd like to introduce you to Max Savage and Sebastian Del Torro, owners of Savage Soho, a three-star Michelin restaurant. Max is married to my cousin, Lucy Dare."

"Lucy *Savage*," Max says in a low, possessive voice.

I smile. "So, you must be related to the Prescotts, too?"

Max, an extremely good-looking man with dark hair, reaches out and shakes my hand. "Yes, we found out we're related." He shrugs, an amused smile on his face.

I grin. I've heard the sperm donor story from my friends Braden and Willow Prescott.

"It's great to meet you, Aurora," Max says.

Sebastian, also an attractive man, steps forward and shakes my hand, as well.

"A pleasure to meet you both," I say.

"So what are you doing here, Max? Did you take up cooking in your spare time?" Nick asks his cousin.

"When I heard you asked Sebastian to put together a special meal, I couldn't resist stopping by to say hello and see who's got you pulling out all the stops." Max glances at me and winks.

I blush but understand.

Nick shrugs, unrepentant. "Well, you've said hello." He slaps the man on the back. "And now you can say goodbye. We'll get together for drinks sometime soon. But tonight, I want to be with my girl."

I open my eyes wide at that claim but possessiveness seems to run in the Dare family.

Max bursts out laughing. "I love it. Have a good night and enjoy. I hope to see you again," he says to me. "I'll let myself out."

"And I'm heading back to the kitchen," Sebastian says. "Are you ready to begin dinner service?"

"Yes, please." Nick waits for the chef to walk back into the kitchen before pulling out the chair at the head of the table. "Have a seat."

I settle in, and he sits next to me.

I'm touched by the lengths to which he's gone for our date. It couldn't be easy for Sebastian to cook in what is a very small area, yet he is here.

"Thank you, Nick. This has been an incredible night."

His eyes gleam with pleasure. "I know you've had the Kingston money for a while now, but I'm sure the fact that you grew up without much is never far from your mind. I just wanted you to feel special."

"I do," I whisper. I take a good look at him, in his

white-collared shirt, unbuttoned enough to reveal a sexy sprinkling of hair. His sleeves are rolled up, his forearms muscular. And his intense gaze bores into mine. He's never made me feel anything but special.

Sebastian chooses that moment to interrupt our mutual scrutiny with a bottle of wine.

Nick and I enjoy a dry white with Sebastian's Chef's Experience menu, which he describes in detail. Through our taste buds, we travel through Spain, sampling the cuisine of the area. It is by and far the best food I've ever had. Eventually, Sebastian says goodnight and leaves us alone.

Nick keeps the conversation light, with most of our talk centered around Leah and her antics. I love telling stories about my daughter, and Nick soaks them up, sometimes laughing. But other times, I catch a sad expression on his face that seems like longing for all he's missed. The look is especially evident when I give him my phone so he can scroll through old photos.

"I have her baby book," I say, just after I've taken my last bite of dessert. "I should have thought to show it to you earlier."

"I look forward to seeing it." He smiles, pushing back his plate. "My family is dying to meet her."

I nod. "I felt bad that we didn't have them at her birthday party."

"It was too soon. Now that she knows I'm her father, I can tell her about my family and prepare her for the sheer amount of Dares she'll soon be meeting," he says, laughing.

I lift my eyebrows. "Why don't you tell *me* about your family?" For all he knows about my past, I know nothing of his.

He pushes back his chair and stands, reaching out his hand to help me stand. "That's a long story. Let's go into the other room, and I'll fill you in."

★   ★   ★

Nick

I PREFER TO live my life in the present, avoiding thinking about my childhood or family history. With my three-date rule and my life on the road, living that way has been easy. But now I have a child and a woman I'm interested in, and they both deserve to know about my very large, very unique family.

"Get comfortable," I say to Aurora. Although I'd rather carry her into the bedroom and bury myself inside her, we aren't there yet.

She sits down on the sofa, and to my surprise, she inches closer, as if she senses my need for her to be within touching distance.

"I know you have a twin sister, and of course I

know Harrison. Who else is there?" she asks.

I stretch my arm along the top of the couch, tangling my fingers in her hair, which grounds me. I look up at the ceiling and gather my thoughts, then start at the beginning. "My dad's name is Michael, and my mother's name was Audrey."

"Was?"

I blow out a harsh breath. "Yeah. She's gone. It's...complicated. To sum up my siblings, there's Asher, who runs Dirty Dare Vodka, and has his hands in a lot of other pies, too. Next is Harrison, who you know, then Zach. He owns a bar in Soho."

I suspect there is more to my independent 'do his own thing' brother than anyone knows. "Then, of course, there's me and Jade, who is the lead Event Coordinator for all the hotels. She lives here in New York."

Aurora tips her head to the side. "Sounds like my siblings. There were four of them until they found me." She looks at me with confusion because I alluded to more family.

And there is.

I rub my fingers along her silky hair. "My mother suffered from mental illness." Now come the uncomfortable parts.

Aurora snuggles into me as I explain. "From what I've been told, she liked to be pregnant, enjoyed the attention she received, but taking care of kids and actually being a mother? Not so much."

Aurora sighs. "That's sad."

"It is. I've only known about Leah for a couple of weeks, but I love the idea of being a part of her life. My mother… She had Asher, and three years later, Harrison. Apparently, she took care of Asher and Harrison as infants but once they were toddlers…" I shake my head, grateful I don't have the memories of neglect in my head that my older siblings have.

Aurora remains silent, but the heat of her body feels good against mine. I never told anyone about my mother before—I never wanted to—but it doesn't surprise me that Aurora makes me feel comfortable to do so.

I swallow hard. "My mother didn't feed or bathe my brothers, so my father hired a nanny. Her name is Serenity. She was eighteen when she moved in. She was from the Midwest, and she was great with all of us. Getting help freed my father to work on convincing Mom to go for professional help."

"Did she?" Aurora asks. She places a hand on my chest, and I nod.

"She went on meds. I don't remember her at all, but Dad and Asher say when she stayed on them, she was okay. But she'd go off them without telling Dad, and sink into a depression. We all lived through cycles like that, until one day, *poof*!" I make a gesture with my hand. "She was gone."

"I'm so sorry," Aurora says.

"Jade and I were only two. Serenity was our constant, thank God. Zach's recollections of Mom are fuzzy. Asher and Harrison, unfortunately, have most of the bad memories." I know I ought to feel more when it comes to my birth mother, but I consider Serenity to be more of a mom than Audrey ever was.

Aurora pushes herself up and shifts positions, one knee beneath her so she can face me. "So your mom suffered from depression?"

"Technically, it was more than that—an actual disorder. It manifests itself in the desire to be pregnant. She loved the attention and would fall into a depression after she gave birth. Dad says he did all he could with birth control except have a vasectomy because she begged him not to. And he loved her too much to go against her wishes."

"I'm sure he was in a difficult position. It's hard to help someone who doesn't want to be helped," Aurora says with an understanding it took me years to find.

"It wasn't like my father gave us intimate details about his marriage. Zach was an accident, of that I'm sure. Then came me and Jade. Twins. Three kids and two infants would have been a handful for someone who *was* mentally stable. My mom didn't stand a chance."

Aurora remains silent, simply letting me talk. So I figure I might as well tell her everything. "The police eventually notified Dad that she'd committed suicide."

Aurora sucks in a startled breath. "Oh my God, I'm so sorry."

I run my knuckles down her cheek. "It's okay. It was a long time ago, and I've come to terms with it."

Although sometimes, I struggle with the fact that Jade has anxiety. She has a handle on it, but I worry about my twin, about whether she could fall into the same hole my mother did. But I don't feel right telling Aurora about Jade's personal issues. "I still haven't told you the *whole* family story."

Aurora bites down on her bottom lip, then releases it. "There's more?"

I laugh, because what else can I do? "Six years after my mom died, Dad married Serenity. And before you ask, I was okay with it. We all were. I mean she raised me. Jade and I call her Mom. My father is a good man and was faithful to our mother, so why begrudge him happiness? He and Serenity lived under one roof. It happened. I have no issues there."

"You love her," Aurora says simply.

"Yeah. She's the only mother I've ever known. I was lucky to have had her in my life."

"Yes, you were," Aurora says, because she knows the alternative better than I do. I hope my past doesn't bring up any pain for her, but she wanted to know, and it feels good to let it all out.

"After a while, Serenity decided she wanted her own kids, not that she ever treated us differently. But she couldn't get pregnant so she underwent fertility treatments." I shake my head and grin. "She had triplets—boys. They're seventeen now. She also had an *oops* baby, and she's twelve. So I have eight siblings…which means Leah has six more uncles and two more aunts. She can even play with some of them. And *that's* my family situation."

Aurora smiles. "Thank you for telling me. Leah will be thrilled."

"I'm glad you feel that way. And I appreciate you giving me the chance to talk about it. You know, from the day we met, I felt like I could say anything to you."

"Yeah?" She sits up on her knees and wraps her arms around my neck, something I take as a good sign.

"I understand that you don't trust easily, and the reasons why. You need to know I didn't bring you here expecting for us to have sex but—"

Before I can finish my sentence, she throws herself into my arms and presses her lips to mine.

CHAPTER SEVEN

Aurora

I ALREADY DECIDED to enjoy tonight and deal with my concerns tomorrow. Nick and I bonded over our painful family histories, and as I look into his eyes, I know I want him.

He stands, urging me to hook my legs around his waist and carries me towards the bedroom. "What are you doing?" I ask, laughing and holding onto him.

"Getting you in bed before you change your mind." He pauses in the doorway of a room that contains a king-sized bed. "You're not having second thoughts, are you?"

I cup his face in my hands. "No, Nick. I want to be with you."

His eyes gleaming with desire, he strides into the room and gently drops me onto the mattress. I lean up on my elbows, watching as he undoes the button on my jeans and lowers the zipper.

He is getting right to it, I think, biting down on my lower lip.

"Lift," he says, and I have no problem following

that order. I raise myself off the mattress, and he wriggles my jeans over my hips and slide them off my legs and onto the floor. My damp panties follow soon after.

He spreads my legs and hooks them over his shoulders, lowering himself so he is eye level with my most intimate parts. Given the choice between squeezing my eyes shut and watching the need etching Nick's handsome features, I choose to observe.

"You're so wet for me," he says in a gruff voice, running a finger over my sex. At his first touch, my hips jerk, and he lets out a pleased groan. "We were so young our first time. We missed out on so much. Tonight, I plan on savoring you." As if to punctuate his words, he dips his head and licks along the seam of my sex.

I arch my back and raise my hips, feeling every swipe and lap of his tongue as he sucks on my outer lips and teases me everywhere. He indulges, feasting, licking, sucking, eating me all over. I love every second he spends making me feel good, but to my frustration, he ignores the spot where I need pressure the most.

I wriggle myself against him, hoping either to give him a hint as to what I want or take what I need myself.

He lifts his head and meets my gaze, his eyes dark with desire. "I know you're trying to control me, but you taste too good. I plan to take my time."

I want to bang my head back on the bed. "I didn't realize you intended to drive me crazy."

He laughs and dives back in, but this time, he flicks my clit with his tongue, tugging and tweaking back and forth, building my pleasure. My vibrator has nothing on Nick's talented moves, and I am so ready to come. My legs tremble as I grind myself against his mouth, trying to get there sooner than he plans.

He slides his tongue along my sex again, parting my wet folds, focusing on my clit, sucking hard. I rub against him, the next swipe of his tongue bringing me higher and closer to what I know will be an explosive orgasm.

But instead of letting me come, he keeps me on the edge, bringing me close…and easing off, then repeating the action.

My body twitches, and I grasp for something just out of reach. "Nick, please."

He lifts his head. "Please what?" he asks, sliding one finger inside me and pumping deep.

I whimper but know he expects an answer. "Please let me come."

He adds a second finger and fills me again, gliding in and out, curling his long digits inside me. He slides along the right spot and presses hard, triggering waves of pleasure that spark outward and take over my entire being.

I cry out, repeating his name as I rock against his mouth to draw out the sensations. White stars flicker behind my eyes, and I might black out for a second, because I realize I've fallen flat on the bed and now struggle to catch my breath.

He rubs his face on my thigh and rises to his feet, undressing, revealing tanned skin and flexing muscles. I push myself up and remove my shirt and bra, tossing them to the floor with the rest of my clothes.

A fully naked Nick places a knee on the mattress and stretches out beside me. "You're gorgeous," he says, his gruff voice arousing me all over again. Who'd have thought I even had it in me to want more? But I still haven't had him inside me. And I desperately want to feel him there.

I press my palms against his strong pecs. "You're pretty impressive yourself."

He leans in and kisses me long and deep, and I melt into his warm, hard body. It is so easy to lose myself in him and forget all the fears that wait for me when I go back to my normal life.

But I promised myself tonight, and I intend to make the most of it.

Nick brushes a strand of hair off my face, his touch gentle. "You know I'm not finished with you tonight, right?"

"No, you're not." I need him to fill the emptiness I've owned for so long.

"What time do you have to be home for Leah?" he asks.

I grin, knowing I am about to make his night. "I don't. Melly said she'd bring her home tonight and stay over, so she could take her to school tomorrow."

In fact, Melly is so pleased I'm going on a date, she did everything she could to make sure I have unlimited freedom.

"And you're just telling me this now?" Nick climbs on top of me.

I shrug, unwilling to admit I've hoped for this all along. "I wanted to see how things played out before I told you." I don't want to give him the impression I'm a sure thing—no doubt, like most other women in his life.

He meets my gaze with a serious expression. "Guess I need to ask you again. Are you changing your mind?"

"Not a chance. But you might when I tell you something." Some men don't want the responsibility of being with a woman who is inexperienced. Back when I was eighteen, and he was only the second guy I had been with, a lack of skill was normal.

But Nick is about to find out I've been with no one else since.

★　★　★

Nick

I STRADDLE AURORA, a knee on either side of her hips, keeping my weight off her. My cock pulses, my desire all consuming. I can't imagine what is on her mind, but it is obviously important.

"There's nothing you could tell me that would freak me out," I assure her.

"Maybe, maybe not," she murmurs, her blue eyes looking into mine.

"Let's hear it, then."

She nods and draws a deep breath. "Okay, well, it's been a long time for me."

Since we're naked, I'm pretty sure I know what she means. I don't like thinking about her with other men, but considering my history, I'd just be happy if she forgets to ask about my past and focuses on hers.

"How long has it been?" I don't want to hurt her, which means I need to know.

Her cheeks flush with embarrassment. I decided she needs a distraction while she tells me. Reaching up, I cupped her breast in my hand and rub one nipple between my two fingers.

She moans and shoots me a dirty look.

I grin but continue to tease her. "How long?" I ask

again, this time in a serious tone.

She purses her lips, then speaks. "You were the last person I was with."

My fingers still. Hell, my entire body grows taut. "Me?"

She nods. "When Leah was conceived."

Our daughter is over five years old. Add another nine months for when Aurora was pregnant. "Six years?"

"Give or take. And if that's too much pressure— you basically being the only one—I understand." She tries to wriggle out from beneath me but I hold her in place.

She told me about her first time. I knew I was her second. To find out there's been no one else since? I'm relieved. Hell, it's a caveman's dream. But she doesn't want an alpha asshole. She wants me to accept her for who she is.

"You probably don't want to hear this, but I'm happy that I was your last guy. I don't like thinking of you with someone else." That notion twists my stomach. "And I'm glad you told me. I don't want to hurt you." I return my focus to playing with her nipple and watching her squirm. "Feel good?" I ask.

"You know it does." She arches her back so her breast pushed against my hand.

I nod my approval. "That means you'll be wet enough."

Her cheeks go from pink to red. "I'm not used to talking about this with anyone."

She is so damned sweet, I want to devour her. Despite her mortification, I already know it doesn't take much to make her forget everything but me.

"Then let's stop talking." I lift my other hand and cup both her breasts, then lean down and pull one distended nipple into my mouth.

Almost immediately, she begins to writhe with pleasure. I intend to get her so worked up, I'll glide right in. My cock pulses at the thought of being enclosed in her wet heat.

I push both her breasts together and switch from one hard bud to the other and back again. I swipe with my tongue and nip with my teeth until she becomes a boneless mess. She grips my waist with her hands, digging her nails into my skin, her hips rocking back and forth. Meaningless noises come from her throat.

"Need something?" I ask, releasing her breasts and sliding a hand to her wet pussy.

"I'm empty," she says, reaching down to grab my cock in her hand.

That quickly, she turns the tables on me. But regardless of how hard I am or how much I need to be inside her, I have to go slowly. I also need to kiss her. I slide my lips over hers, and the kiss I intend to be soft becomes fast and frenzied. We devour each other, making up for lost time.

Rocking my hips, I rub my cock against her slick sex. She moans and claws at my shoulders, grinding herself against me until I know I have to stop or I'll come way too soon.

I break the kiss and lift my head. "I need to grab a condom."

She nods. "I'm on the pill—live and learn. I figured, just in case…" she says. "But since you have super sperm, I won't argue about extra protection."

Chuckling, I push myself off her, walk to the bathroom, and pull a strip of condoms from my dopp kit full of shaving supplies and other items. I rip the foil open and rolled one on before going back to the bed and moving over her.

As her gaze meets mine, my mind returns to our first time, and how I'd been aware, even then, this thing between us was *more*. I brace my hands on either side of her head at the same time her fingers wrap around my cock. Her hand glides up and down my shaft, her grip tightening with each pass.

I groan and with one hand, slide my fingers through her sex, finding her wet and ready for me. I dip my head and kiss her lips, savoring her taste before I line myself up at her entrance and ease inside.

She's tight, and I work my way in, pushing in and gliding out, going deeper with each forward jerk of my hips.

"You feel good," she murmurs, bending her knees to take more of me.

"Fucking heaven," I mutter as I fill her completely.

"I'm good, Nick. Move, or I'm going to lose my mind."

"Thank fuck." I raise my hips, slide out, and began to thrust into her, joining our bodies, beginning an intense rhythm that soon has her crying out.

"Nick, God, harder."

I do as she asks, twisting my hips as I plunge into her.

"Nick!"

Hearing my name on her lips as our bodies connect does something to me. "Again. Say my name." I slide a hand between us and rub her clit, my finger sliding through her wetness.

"Nick!"

I press harder, and she shatters, her inner walls fluttering around me, squeezing me in her heat. I grit my teeth and wait as she rides out her orgasm. When I sense her coming down, I let myself go, picking up the pace and force of my thrusts until I know I'm there.

"Come again," I tell her.

"Can't."

I raise myself up and spear into her again, this time making sure to hit her at the spot I found earlier.

"Oh God!"

"Yes, now come with me," I say, and with a few more targeted thrusts, she screams my name, and I follow her over into utter bliss.

Aurora

I LAY IN Nick's arms, surprised that I've given myself so completely. I deserve this one night, knowing it won't be long before common sense comes roaring back. Right now, though, I am too sated to think clearly. I breathe in his masculine scent and let myself relax.

He runs his hand along my arm. "Do you remember when I got a phone call after Leah's birthday party?"

"Yes." I forgot about it, though, after we told Leah he was her father. Suddenly wary, I pull myself up to a sitting position, wishing we were beneath the covers so I could cover myself.

He sits up, easing his big body against the pillows. "I have to go back to California this week. The issues at the hotel aren't sorting themselves out the way I'd hoped."

"Work is work," I say, hating the disappointment flooding through me. From a rational perspective, I understand. I just wish the abandoned child inside me could accept it as easily.

He reaches out and takes my hand. "You have to know that given a choice, I wouldn't go. But I've been the one dealing with management in our hotels, and situations like the one we have there fall on my shoulders."

I nod. "I get it. When are you leaving?"

"I'll take the jet Tuesday morning. I would have gone today, but I wanted this night with you."

I wanted it, too, but after such an intimate experience with Nick—maybe even because of it—I can't resist the urge to build walls back up around myself. My fear of getting close to a man who pops in and out of my life—and my daughter's life—is back with a vengeance.

I can't sit here naked anymore and go to slide off the bed.

Nick releases my hand and I stand. "I just need to go into the bathroom. I'll be right back." I take a few minutes to myself, splashing my face and washing up before returning to the bedroom. Nick has pulled the covers down and climbed beneath. I take in his broad chest and intense stare, and I can't deny how much I still want him. Whatever this is, I can't take it too seriously. But we are here, so I intend to enjoy it.

He pats the empty spot beside him. "Come back,"

he says in a gruff voice.

I walk over and settle down beside him. He immediately reaches out and pulls me into his arms. Letting myself go, I tuck my chin into the crook between his face and neck and breathe him in. "You smell good," I murmur.

Even his low chuckle is arousing. "You feel even better."

I inhale his masculine scent, my body softens, and I sigh, then hook one leg over his thigh. My sex rubs against his hair-roughened skin, and I moan aloud, enjoying the friction and needing more.

"Isn't this better than overthinking things?" he asks, his thick erection nudging at me.

"Much," I admit.

He flips me onto my back and moves over me, snagging a packet from the nightstand. He separates us long enough to rip the foil and roll the condom over his cock. Without waiting, he edges into me. "I knew you'd be wet enough." He thrusts all the way in, filling me perfectly, as if he is made just for me.

He rocks his hips, his eyes locked on mine, and it doesn't take long before my climax slams into me, and I come with a long, moan. He thrusts harder and deeper, his orgasm triggering another mini one of my own.

Later that night, after we talk about our daughter, I

fall asleep in his arms.

The next morning, after Facetiming with Leah before school, I fall back to sleep, something I never do. Everything about this morning is different from my usual routine. Normally, I wake up to my alarm, have a cup of coffee, put on exercise clothes, and go on the treadmill before taking a quick shower, and waking Leah.

Then, I have breakfast with my chatty child, followed by a rush to the car with me running down a list of things I don't want to forget. Part of me is teaching Leah to think ahead, but a greater part of me just wants to make sure we don't have to take a ride back to kindergarten because we forgot to pack Leah's lunch.

Sleeping in is a luxury, but when I wake up alone in the hotel room at eleven a.m., I am in shock.

I wash up and brush my teeth, then find Nick in the outer room, hunched over a laptop, and drinking coffee. He obviously showered and dressed, looking sexy as ever in a pair of dark jeans and a buttoned-down shirt, with the sleeves rolled up.

"Morning," I say.

"Good morning." He looks me over, his gaze scanning my bare legs beneath the long shirt I put on—his shirt.

"I can't believe you let me sleep in."

His lips lift in a sexy smirk. "You were snoring. I figured you needed it."

I walk over and nudge his shoulder. "I don't snore." A flush of heated embarrassment rises to my cheeks.

"It was adorable," he says, chuckling. "Sit and eat. I ordered muffins so nothing would get cold."

I lower myself into the chair next to him, and since my stomach is rumbling, I choose a large blueberry muffin, pour my coffee and dig in. After I shower and pack up my things, Nick calls for his car, and he drives us back to my house in Old Westbury.

He steps out, comes around and opens my door.

I prep myself to say goodbye. "Well, thank you for an incredible night."

He braces a hand on the top of the window. "That sounds like goodbye."

I raise my eyebrows. "It's not?"

"What do you have planned for the rest of the day?" he asks.

"I have to pick Leah up from school." I'll bring my daughter home, give her a snack, and let her spill all the details about her day while I prep dinner. Then it will be bath time, story time, and bed. But he doesn't need to hear my whole routine.

"Perfect. I was hoping to see Leah. How about we surprise her by picking her up together?"

His eyes light up at the possibility, and I can't mistake the hope in his tone. No way can I deny him the chance to do something so normal for his daughter.

"Sounds like a plan. Come inside. I need to do a few things before it's time to leave."

He accompanies me inside and waits in the family room while I return some work calls that are on my voicemail. I schedule a meeting with Sasha and Cassidy to discuss Billie's idea for FFT, and one with Linc to see what buildings might come up for sale for my housing component. He left a message that he has some leads.

Nick apparently has the same idea because he's on the phone in the family room with what sounds like a business call when I walk in.

He holds up one finger. "Yes. Of course. We'll discuss it all when I get there." He finishes up and disconnects his call. "Ready?" he asks.

I nod. Although his car sits outside, it's a two-seater Porsche.

"I have Leah's car seat in the back of my SUV. Come on," I say. I start for the garage entrance and realize Nick isn't behind me. I walk back to the family room where he stands in what appears to be shock. "What's wrong?"

"I didn't know a five-year-old needed a car seat."

In an effort not to laugh because he seems so horrified, I bite down on the inside of my cheek. "Actually, it's a booster seat, but yeah. She needs one, and she can't ride in a two-seater."

He blows out a breath and shakes his head. "I have a lot to learn and buy," he mutters, gesturing for me to go to the garage.

I laugh and walk out. He'll get it eventually. If Nick Dare is anything, it is determined.

We pick up Leah from school. She's delighted to see Nick and all but ignores me as she dives into his arms and lets him pick her up and carry her to the car. He lifts her up high so she can chatter in his ear as we walk.

No sooner are we all settled in the car than Nick asks, "Who wants ice cream?"

Ice cream. Talk about screwing with our 'let's go home, be calm, have a snack, and wind down' routine. Once Leah screams yes, I can't say anything—not yet. I have no intention of being the bad guy. But Nick and I *will* talk later.

After ice cream, we go to a playground at a nearby park. Nick pushes Leah on a swing, sending her so high I nearly throw up my ice cream.

Once back at the house, I give up. I let Nick's offer of pizza happen and put the chicken I took out earlier to defrost back in the refrigerator for another night. I bathe our daughter, and while Nick reads her a bedtime story, I walk into the kitchen and pour myself a glass of wine.

I don't drink often but tonight, I need to take the edge off. Everything about Nick being around today messed with my head. My routines are off, and as a single mom, I live and die by my routines. Not only do they make life easier, but they give Leah the security that I, myself, had never had.

Depending on the foster home I was in at the time, I didn't know what I would be coming home to after school. Sometimes, I might find my foster mom, a day drinker who managed to hide it well from social services, passed out on the couch. In another home, I was never sure if there would be dinner on the table. If I was lucky, sometimes I found enough food to make a sandwich myself. But that often wasn't the case.

There were no bedtime stories for me. No safe baths. I make sure my daughter has it all.

One day with Nick upended the security I've given Leah. I take a sip of the dry wine and shake my head, knowing I'm lying to myself. Being with Nick is good for my daughter.

What Nick upends is my own sense of security. And I'm not sure what I am going to do about that.

Nick

WHEN I JOIN Aurora in the kitchen, she's staring at her wine glass, swirling the golden liquid. I had the best couple of days and didn't think anything could bring me down. I had a night with Aurora that was spectacular. Being with her again reminds me why no other woman has managed to capture my interest. I spent the late afternoon and tonight with my daughter, learning about her likes, dislikes, looking through her baby book with her before she fell asleep.

I've been riding a high until I walk into this room and see Aurora's pensive expression. Even after a long day, she's so damned pretty. But she doesn't look as happy as I've been feeling. My heart squeezes in my chest, but I refuse to open the conversation on a negative note.

"Today was perfect." I step into the kitchen, and she jerks in her seat, just realizing I'm here.

"Want some wine?" she asks, gesturing to the bottle with an empty glass beside it.

I shake my head. "No, thanks."

"Is Leah asleep?"

I can't stop my grin. "Yeah. Conked out while telling me she couldn't wait for her first visit from the tooth fairy so you could tape her tooth into the baby book."

Aurora smiles and shudders at the same time. "I don't think I'll do well with a dangling tooth. I've heard horror stories from some of Leah's friends' moms."

I grin. "I can handle that."

"Right. And you'll leave a hundred-dollar bill under her pillow, no doubt." I catch the bite in her tone.

I walk into the room and sit down beside her. "What's wrong?" I ask.

She turns to face me. "I am so glad you spent today with us. I'm even happier Leah had such a great time."

"But?" Because I sense a big one.

She rubs her palms along the stem of her glass. "For so long, it was just me and Leah. Yes, I had family, and when I lived with Melly, I was so lucky to have had help. But two years ago, I decided to move out. And Leah and I...we're a team. She knows what to expect every day and that's something I never had."

I don't pacify her with platitudes like, *I'm here now*, or *you're not alone anymore*. I listen. Really listen and try to understand what she's getting at. "Are you saying I'm intruding?" The thought makes me physically ill.

"No." She shakes her head. "God, no." Reaching out, she grasps my hand and electricity darts through me, reminding me of being buried deep inside her and knowing we are meant to be. "But I am saying that today was an anomaly, and not just because you wreaked havoc with my routine."

A smile plays around those luscious lips and the twisting in my gut eases a little. "I took over and made things big again?"

"That's part of it. There's nothing wrong with surprise ice cream after school. Or the playground. Or pizza for dinner. But maybe not all on the same day. Parents need to agree before offering up those things. Or one day, she's going to do an end run around me because she knows Daddy will say yes."

She pulls back her hand and reluctantly, I let her go. Her words hit home, and I understand. "I should have discussed it with you first."

She nods. "That's part of it. Being a parent...it doesn't come with a rule book. You'll learn."

"What else?"

She draws a deep breath. "You're not always going to be here. That's the nature of your job, your life."

I open my mouth to speak but she holds up a hand. "It's okay. We both know what the reality is. But I don't want her to resent me for being strict, because when you come around, it's all fun and games."

I nod, taking in her words and understanding. She isn't wrong. This is my life, at least for now. "I get it.

I'm glad I had today but I'll learn."

She nods as she takes a sip of her wine.

Watching her, I drum my fingers against the granite counter. I know her better than she thinks, and there is more. She wasn't staring into her wine glass about today's adventures alone. "That's not all that's bothering you."

She sighs and places the glass on the counter. "You're right." Her light blue eyes stare into mine. "This is hard to explain. Hard to say." She hesitates, and I give her time to gather her thoughts. "I've been on my own for a long time and I've been in survival mode even longer, first for myself and then for myself and Leah. All I ever wanted was to give Leah the stability I never had."

"And you think I threaten that somehow." I lean an elbow on the hard granite.

"I think you threaten me and the life I've built for us. But not for the reason you might think. It's not because Leah suddenly has her father in her life that I feel this way—I want that for her. And I want you to be a part of Leah's future. But instability makes me anxious. The coming and going at the whim of a phone call? That's hard for me."

I know how difficult that is for her to admit, and I put my hand over hers this time and brush my thumb over her soft skin. I'm not sure what to say or promise in order to reassure her. She's right. I have a job that keeps me on the move, and I don't see that changing any time soon. But that doesn't mean I can't be a permanent fixture in Aurora and Leah's lives.

"I'm going to do my best to get up to speed as a parent," I promise her.

Her lips twitch, but her smile is genuine. "I know you will and I'm sure you'll be a fast study."

"I appreciate that." I want to say more, but it would only be rehashing what she's already said.

I know her fears, and I need to think about what I can do to make things work between us. Early on, I was overly optimistic that sheer determination would win her over and get me what I want. Us as a family…on my terms. I realize my mistake now.

"Look, it's been a long day and I'm sure you're exhausted."

"And you need to get ready for your trip," she says.

I nod. "I do." I rise from my seat and hold out my hand. "Walk me to the door?"

She slides her palm against mine and follows me through the main area of the house, to the front entrance.

Although I feel like we're at an impasse, we still made progress over the last couple of days. I'm not going to let her minimize our connection.

So I slide my hand around her waist and yank her against me.

She lets a surprised gasp but doesn't pull away. Instead, she wraps her arms around me, too, her hands settling on my hips.

"Be good while I'm gone," I say in a gruff voice, knowing I'll miss her, no matter how long or short a time I'm gone.

"Be good while you're away."

"Always," I say, and capture her mouth, sliding my tongue inside her parted lips.

She moans and tightens her grip on my waist, letting me back her against the nearest wall as my mouth plunders hers. I need a thorough taste to hold me over until my return. I taste a hint of wine and everything Aurora and my cock throbs, urging me to take her upstairs to her room. But that can't happen—not now. She has a lot to think about, and I've pushed her far enough tonight. Not to mention, our daughter is home, and I have no idea how to handle that with care.

I break the kiss but keep her backed to the wall, held there by my body.

"Good night."

"Night, Nick." She licks at her now swollen lips.

I step away from her and let myself out into the dark night, feeling optimistic.

Yeah, I've given her plenty of memories in the last couple of days. Hopefully, it will be enough to compete with her fears.

CHAPTER EIGHT

Aurora

ROUTINE KEEPS ME busy while Nick is gone. Routine. It isn't something I've given much thought to until Nick entered our lives. But as I told him, keeping to a schedule keeps me sane and teaches Leah to be responsible. But I can't deny I enjoyed my day of fun with Nick and Leah. We were like a family, something I never had. And although Nick has reappeared, it still, somehow, feels out of reach. At least for me.

Nick Facetimes often from California in a way I can count on—first, during Leah's breakfast in the morning, even if it means he has to wake up at an ungodly hour in L.A. and then around four p.m. during Leah's down time after school. He's also added a third time, around nine-thirty, right before I turn in for bed.

Tonight, I slide under the covers, my bare legs feeling the cool sensation of the sheets against my skin. Leah is tucked into bed, and two glasses of water to quench her thirst later, she is sleeping like a baby.

I tip my head against the pillows and sigh. It was a busy but productive week at work. I breathe in deep and focus on some relaxation techniques when my phone rings.

Knowing who it is, I answer without checking the screen. "Hi, Nick."

"Hi, yourself."

I take in his deep, rich voice. "No Facetime tonight?"

He chuckles. "No. I was at the gym in the hotel and I'm on my way back to my room to shower before dinner. I have a meeting with the new manager and his assistant in an hour. Then I can leave in the morning, as planned."

My heart skips a beat. "So you're coming home? I mean back to New York?" He doesn't have a home to speak of.

"Yes. I'm coming *home*." He pauses, and I know he's letting the word linger between us. "Would you be up to bringing Leah to my parents' place in Greenwich on Saturday? My family would love to meet you both."

I knew the time was coming, but I can't deny how nervous I am at the thought of facing his family. What if they blame me for keeping Leah from Nick? Or they don't like me? I already know they'll love Leah. Of course, I'm biased, but I know the truth—my kid is awesome.

But why do I care so much what Nick's family will think, anyway?

"Hey. Are you breathing, or did you pass out on me?" Nick asks, his tone calming.

He's not laughing at me.

"I'm here. Sure. That's fine."

"They're going to love you both," he says, as if reading my thoughts. "And they know the facts. That you really had no way of finding me when you realized you were pregnant. They're going to make you feel like one of us. I promise."

How does he always read me so well?

"Okay," I say, letting out the breath I've been holding before I grow dizzy.

"I'll come and get you, myself."

I frown. "But my place is in the opposite direction. You'll be driving twice as long."

He lets out a low chuckle. "How much more nervous will you be if you have to meet me there?" he asks.

The thought churns my stomach, and I can't reply.

"Point made. I'll come out Saturday morning."

I know he's grinning, and somehow it calms me. "Thanks."

"Is Leah asleep?" he asks.

"One story and two glasses of water and yes, she's sleeping."

"I'm looking forward to reading her a story again.

And I really can't wait to see *you*." His voice sounds like smooth whiskey, and my body responds, softening with need. "And on that note, I'll let you get to bed."

"Nick?" I ask.

"Hmm?"

I draw a deep breath. "Thank you." I sense he'll know what for without me spelling it out.

"Anything for you. Now get some sleep."

His low, sexy voice rumbles through me, arousing me to the point where I wonder if I'll have to use my vibrator before I calm down enough to sleep.

"Dream about me," he says and disconnects the call.

I roll over and open my nightstand drawer, knowing I'll do more than dream about Nick.

★ ★ ★

Nick

I PULL AURORA'S SUV into the driveway of my parents' house and shut off the engine. Set back from the street, the structure is ten thousand square feet, massive in size. If I didn't know Aurora lived at the Kingston estate for a number of years, I'd be concerned she'll be intimidated by the home I grew up in.

What *does* concern me however, is the likelihood

that she'll be overwhelmed by the amount of family who might show up today. All my siblings have been invited. I decided to arrive early to ease Aurora and Leah into the chaos.

Obviously excited, Leah has chattered the entire trip, not giving me a chance to talk to Aurora in any meaningful sense. The only way I know what is going on in her head is by the way she is twisting her hands in her lap.

"Are we here?" Leah asks.

Aurora releases her hands and turns. "We are. Are you ready?"

"Yes!" Leah exclaims.

Well, at least one of us is excited. I glance at Aurora, about to reassure her but she's already stepped out of the car. I climb out and go to get Leah, opening her door.

She's already unbuckled her seatbelt and is halfway out of her booster seat without help.

"That's some outfit," I say to Aurora, who's joined me.

I recognize Leah's leggings as Burberry. They are paired with a hot pink flowered top I'm not sure match the pants. And a headband with…yes, a big pink flower, sits on her head, and white sneakers are on her feet.

"It was a gift from Chloe. Way more than I would

have spent, but I appreciated the sentiment. I told Leah it was for special occasions and today she used those words against me. She declared it was an important day and she needed to look pretty."

I laugh. My kid is smart.

Aurora shrugs. "I learned a long time ago to pick my battles." Her gaze slides to our daughter, and she smiles wide. "Besides, she really does look cute."

I grin. "She sure does."

She shifts her grip on the present she insisted on bringing for my parents.

"Can I take that for you?" I hold out my hands.

She shakes her head. "It's not heavy."

"Are you ready? You okay?"

She lifts her sunglasses and props them on top of her head. "I'm fine. Honestly."

I look into her pretty sky-blue eyes and believe her. "Just to say, in case I haven't already, you look gorgeous."

My gaze skims over her off-white, tapered pants, Chanel sandals, and a royal blue satin top, with flirty ruffles on the short sleeves, that accentuate her eyes. I know, without asking, that she's spent a long time choosing her outfit in order to make a good impression on the people I care about.

"Let's go!" Leah tugs on my hand.

I look at Aurora. "You heard her. Let's go," I say

just as Leah begins to skip up the path.

I place a hand on Aurora's lower back and lead her across the large bluestones and to the front door. Leah lifts her hand to ring the bell, but the door opens before she can push, and Serenity appears.

A wide smile graces her face but Leah takes a step back and is suddenly shy. Before I can introduce anyone, my father walks up beside his wife.

I am proud, as I say, "Dad, Mom, this is Aurora, and our daughter, Leah."

★　★　★

Aurora

I STUDY NICK'S parents, struck by how much Nick looks like his father. Michael's dark hair has very few streaks of gray, and he possesses the same indigo blue eyes as Nick and Leah, as well as similar features. Looking at Nick's father gives me a good idea of how well Nick will age.

I've seen pictures of my own father at Melly's, but I don't have any of my own. And since I was too young when my grandmother died to understand about holding onto mementos like photographs, I have none of my mother, either. Not that I consider my parents keepsake-worthy.

"Aurora, meet my parents, Serenity and Michael Dare," Nick says.

"It's a pleasure," I murmur, one hand holding the gift, the other I place on my daughter's head.

"The same here," Michael says. "We've heard so much about you both."

"And this is Leah." Nick reaches for our little girl and she lets go of my pants and grasps her father's, making my throat grow thick with emotion. It is amazing to see how quickly she's taken to and accepted Nick.

Michael steps forward and crouches down, bringing him eye level with his granddaughter. "Hi, Leah. I'm your daddy's daddy. Do you know what that means?"

The usually loud child shakes her head in silence.

"I'm your grandpa, and Serenity is your grandma."

The beautiful woman with long black hair smiles at Leah but stays back, obviously giving her time to adjust.

"Like Grandma Melly?" Leah asks.

I smile. "Exactly like Grandma Melly."

Leah seems to think about that. "Okay."

"God, I wish being an adult was that easy," Michael says, rising to his feet and putting an arm around his wife.

Serenity grins. "Nothing in life is easy, but it's all

Just One Dare

worth it. Now that the uncomfortable introductions are out of the way, come in and make yourselves at home," she says, kissing Nick's cheek. "Good to see you."

"You, too," he says. "Where is everyone?"

"Jade is in the kitchen. She's the only one here already. The triplets are at their friends' house. At their age, it's all they want to do, and we thought it would be easier if we didn't overwhelm you," Serenity says. "There will be enough adults, as it is. But Layla is home. She's twelve. I figured that would be an easy enough meet."

"Good thinking," Nick says.

"Thank you," I say. Serenity is so kind. Nick hit the jackpot getting her as his stepmom.

Michael looks at Nick, then Leah. "How about we go inside and you can meet your...meet Layla." He chuckles. "Seems odd to call Layla an aunt right now."

Everyone laughs.

"Come on, princess." Nick pulls Leah to him. "Let's go meet my sister." He glances at me, silently asking if I'll be okay with Serenity.

I give him a subtle nod.

"Aurora, we can go hang out in the kitchen. Jade wants to meet you. And Nick told us about your charity. I'd love to hear more about it," Serenity says, gesturing for me to follow.

I blink in surprise. Nick told his parents about my job? "Sure." I glance down at the gift in my hand. "Oh! This is for you." I hand the wrapped box to Serenity. "It's just a little something to say thank you for having us."

The other woman studies me, her expression gentle. "Thank you, Aurora. But from now on? No gifts like you're some stranger or outsider. You're family, you hear?" Serenity accepts the present, and we walk into the kitchen. "Although I have to say, I love presents," she murmurs as she sets it on the counter. "I'll open it later. I want to talk, first."

I like this woman already.

"Hi, Aurora." A pretty woman who has to be Jade walks over. She has blonde hair and Nick's indigo blue eyes, filled with warmth. She pulls me into an unexpected hug. "I'm so happy to meet you." Releasing me, Jade steps back. "It's brave of you to come deal with the masses all at once."

I laugh. "The Kingstons are pretty much the same. I'm prepared."

Serenity chuckles. "Let's sit."

I sit down on a bar stool and place an elbow on the white and light gray veined granite island and glance around. The appliances are top of the line stainless steel. My kitchen is beyond anything I ever dreamed I would have, but this is a step above.

"The house is beautiful, but this room is incredible," I say. My gaze falls on a coffee maker set into the backsplash across the room, next to the sink. Each look around shows me something new.

Serenity takes a seat. "Thank you. I picked everything. I love to cook, so I was fussy about what I chose. With so many kids, I also wanted things practical. Like these stools? Faux leather, easy to clean."

"Even with one child, I understand. Spills happen all the time. But I'm more of a basic cook. I didn't learn until a couple of years ago." I blush as I realize I've alluded to my embarrassing childhood.

Nick's family might have their issues, but nobody dumped their kid in foster care and ignored them for eighteen years.

"How well you cook doesn't matter as long as you eat together, right? Besides, there's always mac and cheese."

"That there is." I appreciate how easy it is to talk to Nick's stepmother.

"I love mac and cheese," Jade says. "You used to make it for us all the time." She glances at Serenity and smiles before turning back to me. "I'm looking forward to having another woman at these family gatherings."

Serenity nods. "Agreed."

They're going out of their way to make me feel

welcome, and I'm so grateful. "Thank you."

Serenity brushes at a piece of lint on her blouse. "Michael and I are so happy you and Nick reconnected. It would have been a tragedy for the three of you never to have become a family."

Serenity's point hits home, and I find myself confiding in them both. "I'd always regretted that Leah would never know her father. When I saw Nick across the room at the premiere, I was shocked, and it took a little while to sink in, but I knew knowing her father was everything I'd ever wanted for Leah."

Serenity smiles. "I've never seen Nick so happy or complete and I have no doubt it's because he has *both* of you in his life."

"It's true," Jade murmurs. "He's lucky things have worked out. As for me, I'm on a man-fast."

I can't help but grin. "Watch it. I said the same thing before Nick burst into our lives." Realizing what I've implied, I feel my face heat. "I mean, not that Nick and I are…well I don't know what Nick and I are." I swallow hard. "But you're tempting fate."

Serenity puts a hand on Jade's shoulder. "She's right. Just because you've had two duds, that doesn't mean the third time won't be the charm."

I raise my eyebrows, unsure of what they're talking about. But I don't think it's my place to ask.

"I know, you're curious." Jade purses her lips.

"I've had two broken engagements and currently believe all men are assholes," Jade admits.

"Jade Dare. Language!" Serenity shakes her head, but I catch her grin.

"Mom here just thinks she has to guide us. Her language can be as bad as mine."

I pull in a deep breath, deeply affected by Jade and her stepmom's easy relationship. I don't know Jade's feelings about her own mother, but it's clear that like Nick, Jade thinks of Serenity as her mom, in every sense of the word.

It's also obvious that Jade has been hurt by bad relationships and has built barriers around her emotions—something I recognize all too well. I like Nick's sister and hope we can be friends.

The doorbell rings, and the next thing I know, family surrounds me. I'm introduced to the rest of the Dare clan as they trickle into the house and make their way into the kitchen. Asher is missing, apparently called away on business at the last minute. It seems to be a family theme, I think.

For a while, Nick and Harrison help make me comfortable around their other siblings by introducing me, staying by my side, and telling stories about Nick growing up. I appreciate their thoughtfulness, but Nick's family is easy to relax around. They aren't pretentious and make me feel like one of them.

Serenity even catches up with me again to ask questions about Future Fast Track, truly interested in the details.

Leah seems to be having a blast with her "aunt" Layla, and meeting her family. She's passed around, always the center of attention. They all brought gifts for Leah and for Layla, which makes Leah extremely happy, and easily wins her over. Instead of her being overwhelmed, Leah and I fit in. I'm sure the size of the Kingston clan has us used to the large family dynamic.

"Why do we always end up in this room?" Michael complains, as he pours himself a glass of soda. "We have a perfectly good family room with much more comfortable chairs."

"The food is here. Where else should we be?" Harrison asks, then glances at me and winks.

That gesture has Nick appearing at my side, letting me know without words that he's been keeping an eye on me. I can't deny how much I like knowing he cares enough to make sure I'm okay. And I like to see that he can be jealous, even if his brother is just being sweet.

"Relax, Dad. This is what we do," Jade says. "You should be used to it." She wraps an arm around Michael and kisses his cheek. He hugs her in return.

At the innocent, every day gestures, my heart

squeezes tight. I never knew that acceptance and love from my own parents. I never will.

"Hey. Are you okay?" Nick asks.

The pain in my chest eases. "I am. Your family is great." I hesitate and decide to be honest. "I thought the Kingstons and their big, happy family were an anomaly. But you all are showing me that it can be the norm." And I missed out on so much more than I imagined growing up.

Nick clasps my hands in his, and I soak up his warmth. "The Kingstons are *your* big, happy family. You're not an outsider. Not to them."

I blink in surprise. "I didn't realize I was referring to them that way."

They are the family who found me, who took me in, who gave me money they said belonged to me, and they accepted me. But until now, I didn't realize how much I think of the family as *them*…and myself, as a separate entity.

"Did I say something wrong?" Nick asks.

I shake my head. "Not at all. You gave me something to think about," I murmur.

"Hey, little brother." Zach, a big man, dressed in faded jeans and a battered motorcycle jacket, joins us. "I haven't had time to meet your woman."

His interruption comes just in time, before I can get caught up in thoughts of the past. But… *His woman?* "I'm not...we're not..."

"We are," Nick says, sliding an arm around my waist in a slick move. "But you'll have to forgive Zach. He's the Neanderthal of the family. It's the company he keeps."

"Oh, you have plenty of Neanderthal in you, too." I pointedly glance at Nick's hold on my waist, and he squeezes tighter.

I can't deny his possessiveness turns me on, something I don't want to think about around his family.

I focus on Zach. "You own a bar?" I ask the handsome man, who has shaggy hair and a healthy scruff of beard.

"Among other pursuits," he says vaguely. He grins, and I immediately know Zach Dare has secrets. "You two made one adorable kid."

"Yeah, we did."

I love the warmth in Nick's tone when he speaks of our daughter.

"I think so, too, but thank you," I say.

"Mom, Mom, Mom!" As if on cue, Leah comes running in, but before Nick can grab her, Zach scoops her into his arms. "Mom!" she yells once more.

"Yes! Right here. What's up?" I ask.

"Uncle Zach got me Unicorn Poo!" Leah's excitement is palpable, but I shake my head.

"You got her what?" I ask, envisioning something

I'll have to clean up after.

"You heard the lady. Unicorn Poo." Zach treats me to an unrepentant grin.

"What the he…heck, man?" Nick obviously catches his word choice in front of his daughter.

"Relax. They're bath bombs, right, kid?" Zach juggles Leah in his arms and she giggles, then he puts her back down on the floor.

"Leah, come have a snack," Serenity calls, and Leah darts over to where her new grandmother stands by a plate of cookies.

Nick turns to his brother. "What do you know about bath bombs?" he asks, obviously confused. Based on Zach's un-dad-like appearance, I know why.

"One of the waitresses has a daughter Leah's age. I asked her what a good gift would be." Zach shrugs. "Easy."

"So you chose Unicorn Poo." I shake my head, laughing.

"Gotta be the cool uncle."

Nick rolls his eyes. "You think you're cool, huh?"

"Compared to Mr. Three Dates and I'm Out? Yeah, I'm the cool one."

"Umm, *what*?" I glance from Zach to Nick. "Three dates? What does that mean?" I have no idea what to make of Zach's comment.

Nick glares at his brother.

"And on that note, I'm gone." Zach takes my hand. "Great meeting you. I'm sure I'll see you soon." He leans in and brushes a friendly kiss on my cheek. "Don't kill him for who he used to be," he whispers in my ear.

And then the enigmatic brother is gone, leaving me with questions I won't get answered while surrounded by people. And not on the ride home, either, as Leah repeats her interactions with every relative she met until she passes out. But I'll find out. Soon.

★　★　★

Nick

I PARK THE SUV in Aurora's garage and shut off the engine.

"Are we home?" Leah asks.

"I thought she was asleep?" I ask.

Aurora turns to glance at the child in the back. "She sensed the car shutting off. We're home but it's late. Bath and bed."

"Can we use the Unicorn Poo in the bath?" Leah asks, unbuckling herself and opening the car door.

We exit the vehicle, and I know enough to let Aurora handle things tonight.

"It's late. Let's save Uncle Zach's gift for tomorrow. You can even skip a bath now and take one in the morning with the bath bombs, if you like. But you have to promise to go right to sleep."

"Yes!" Leah raises a victorious hand in the air, and as Aurora shuts the electric garage door and opens the door to the house, Leah darts inside.

I step up behind Aurora, my mouth close to her ear. "Good call, Mom."

Her body trembles, and she turns to face me. "You're trouble, Nick."

"Only for you." I back her against the door frame. "Today was successful, wouldn't you say?" My goal is to stay the night, but I have no idea where her head is.

"I'd say so. Everyone was kind and welcoming. You're very lucky to have them all," she says.

"I am." Seeing her fit in with my family cements what I already know—we are meant to be together, and not only because we have a child. If she lets me, I'll make her a part of my family, the way the Kingstons had made her part of theirs.

She just has to realize where—and with whom—she belongs.

She steps inside, and I follow, the house door closing behind us. Before she can head upstairs, I catch her hand, and she turns to face me.

"Ask me," I say.

She wrinkles her nose in question. "Ask you what?"

I bracket her against the nearest wall. "No games. Ask me about the three-date shit Zach mentioned." I know how bad it sounds.

I saw her reaction and sense that is the reason she's been so quiet on the way home. But my explanation will go a long way towards smoothing out the rough waters between us.

She sighs. "Fine. I was going to ask anyway. What did Zach mean by three dates and you're out? Is that how you treated women?"

"Here's the thing. I dated. If I found a woman I could see a future with, I would have kept seeing her. But I always knew within three dates if that was even a possibility." I shrug because I never set out to hurt anyone. "It made sense to me. Why string someone along if I knew it wasn't going to work?"

She narrows her gaze, her sensual lips pursed in thought. "So you really have that rule?"

"I did. But not any longer. Because I found you again. You're the only woman with whom I could ever envision having more. Even after that first night." I touch my forehead to hers. "I came back the next day, remember?"

"Yes," she whispers.

"Now ask me why no one ever got past three dates." I breathe in the lingering scent of her vanilla-based perfume, and my cock gets hard.

"Why?" she asks.

I raise my head and bring my hand up, cupping her jaw. "Because none of them were you," I say. Then I lower my lips and capture hers.

Her mouth is warm and welcoming, and I drink her in, kissing her, licking at her lips, my tongue tangling with hers. More. I want more. And by the way her hands slide into my hair, holding my head in place, I can tell she does, too.

"Mommy! I'm stuck!" Leah screams from upstairs.

I break our connection. "Little cockblocker," I say, laughing.

Aurora grins. "I should go help her."

I take her hand. "Tell me I can stay tonight," I say, as she moves to go up the stairs.

Her gaze meets mine, and the seconds tick away in silence. I wait while she obviously thinks things through.

"You can stay," she says at last.

"Mommy!"

I shake my head and grin. "We forgot the presents in the car. I'll grab them while you go rescue her."

An hour later, thanks to my little negotiator, Aurora and I stand in the hallway outside Leah's bedroom. Earlier, she got her head stuck in her pajamas, hence the call for help. Then, since there was no bath, Leah wheedled us into telling her two stories, one from

Aurora, then one from me, with a glass of water in between. She has a routine, just the way her mother likes it.

It was a great day. Still, I'm glad when Leah falls asleep mid-final story…and I finally have Aurora alone.

CHAPTER NINE

Aurora

T HE DAY HAS been a long one for me. Tiring and enlightening. Overwhelming and frightening. But ultimately satisfying.

Nick's earlier words, *because none of them were you,* stay with me. When I truly consider what he meant, I realize that I need to open myself up to him or I'll lose what I am starting to realize is a good man.

I close Leah's door, leaving it open enough so my daughter can see the glow of the nightlight from the hall, and I can hear Leah, if the little girl calls out.

I blow out a breath and turn to Nick, holding out my hand.

He entwines my fingers with his. "Where to?"

I consider bringing him to the family room but then decide, why delay the inevitable? If I'm in, I might as well be all in.

"My room."

His eyes gleam with desire. "Lead the way, beautiful."

I lead him to my bedroom and step inside the

place that has always been my sanctuary—complete with a king-sized bed, a white fluffy comforter and pillows, and pastel paintings on the walls. No man has ever been inside this room before Nick.

"You can shut the door and lock it, if you'd like. Before we go to sleep, we'll open it again," I say.

Nick does as I say, and pushes the button on the doorknob. The click reverberates through my body.

"I'm not sure if it's a good idea for Leah to find us in bed together tomorrow," I say, facing him.

He steps forward and cups my face in his hands. "Then I'll make sure I'm up before she wakes up. Just let me know what time."

"Seven," I say, seconds before his mouth comes down on mine. The kiss isn't slow or gentle—it is hot and full of need.

Still kissing me, he walks me backwards until my legs hit the mattress and I collapse on the bed.

He lifts his head and reaches for the buttons on his shirt. "Strip," he says, his gruff tone causing my panties to get wetter.

It's hard to concentrate on removing my own clothes when I'm so busy watching him reveal his tanned, muscular skin. I try not to drool as he undoes his shirt and lets it fall to the floor. He kicks off his shoes and pulls off his socks, then his hands move to his pants.

He undoes the button when his eyes meet mine. "Do you like watching me?"

I nod and push his hands out of the way so I can unzip his fly, then hook my fingers in his waistband and pull off his pants, taking off his boxer briefs along with them. I suck in a deep breath as his hard cock bobs close to my face.

He stands watching me, hands clenched at his sides.

He is so gorgeous, he takes my breath away. But I've always been too preoccupied with my doubts to fully enjoy him. Tonight, I intend to do just that.

I wrap my hand around his cock, exploring the rigid thickness as my hand slides up and down his hard length.

A low moan reverberates from deep in his throat and precome forms at the head. Tempted, I lower myself to my knees, intending to attempt something I've read about in books but have never done myself. He doesn't seem to realize my inexperience, or even care, if the sound he makes is anything to go by.

He rests his hand on the top of my head as I open my mouth and draw him in. His taste is salty, his scent musky, and as I slide my tongue along the underside of his erection, I feel him swell in my mouth.

He lets out a low groan. "God, that's good. Keep going," he urges, twisting my hair in his hand and tugging, urging me on.

Knowing I am giving him pleasure causes an erotic thrill, and I squeeze my thighs together, feeling a wave of need wash over me. It isn't intense yet, but that will come…after he does.

I begin to suck, moving my mouth up and down his shaft, and his hips thrust along with me. He shifts his hand lower, gripping the back of my scalp, and pulls my hair with every jerk of his lower body.

His large cock hits the back of my throat and my eyes tear up but I don't stop. His groans and rough encouragement excite me, and I can sense him losing control. I pick up my tempo and with my other hand, I cup his balls in my hand.

"Fu-uck," he mutters and pulls himself back.

I release his shaft with a pop and look up at him. "What's wrong?"

"Not a damned thing." He brushes a finger beneath my damp eyes. "Get undressed so I can come inside you."

My lips part, and I nod.

As quickly as possible, I rise and strip naked, tossing my clothes onto the floor. His hot gaze rakes over me. With a groan of approval, he picks me up and places me on the bed. He snags a condom from his jeans pocket and rolls it on, then stretches out beside me.

I barely have time to blink when he sits up and grabs me, settling me on my knees astride him.

"Ride me, beautiful."

I don't think, just grip his cock in my hand, and lower myself onto him. As he slides inside, I feel every inch of him filling me. I begin to move up and down, repeating the motion, over and over, connecting us in the most intimate way.

His hot gaze locks on mine, and everything I feel for him flows through me. The longing, the wanting, the need accumulates inside me and a lump rises in my throat. I shut my eyes, wanting to push away the depth of emotion our joining causes.

"Eyes open," he says sharply.

Before I can react, he raises his lower body off the mattress and flips us, so he's on top and in control. He braces his hands on either side of my head, his strong body over mine.

"What you feel…" he says, thrusting in and out of me, his intent stare holding mine in a way I can't deny or shut out. "This is us." His thick erection anchors so deep inside me, I'm afraid he's reaching my heart.

I gasp and can't look away.

"It's never been like this for me. Only with you," he says. And then he begins to take me hard, shifting his hips with each thrust until he hits *that* spot. The one that has me seeing stars. Hell, I'm flying so high, I see the entire universe.

My orgasm hits, and I barely recognize the sound I make. "Nick, God, more!" I dig my fingers into his shoulders, and he works as I ride out my climax.

Just when I come down, his orgasm wracks his body above me, and he groans. "Fuck. I love you." He stiffens as he comes, warmth flowing inside me along with too many feelings for me to name.

I don't know how much time passes before I open my eyes. Nick rolls off me, walks to the bathroom and returns.

He helps me clean up and pulls me against him, his arm around my body, holding me tight.

"Nick, about what you said…"

He grunts in my ear. "We aren't going to discuss it now," he says in a gruff voice. "You're going to tell me in your time, when you're ready."

That lump returns to my throat because I do love him. How can I not? But he's right. I'm not ready to say it yet.

I need to have all of my shit together and be ready before I say those words. It has to be perfect.

I curl against him, my head on his chest, and I fall into a deep sleep.

Aurora

I GROAN AND roll over, realizing Nick is gone. As promised, he woke up early enough to avoid having Leah find him in my bed.

What time is it, anyway? After a glance at my phone, I bolt up in bed. Eight thirty! I rush to the bathroom, take care of things, wash up and brush my teeth. Then I pull on an old tee-shirt, a pair of panties and shorts before going to see why Leah hasn't woken me. Leah isn't in bed, which doesn't make sense. She always wakes up early and climbs into my bed for snuggle time.

The sound of voices directs me to the kitchen where Nick and Leah are…making breakfast? Stunned, I stand in the entrance and watch in silence.

"Hand me the bacon but stay away from the hot stove," Nick says.

"Here!" Leah smacks him in the arm with a strip of bacon.

I wince, but Nick doesn't miss a beat. He accepts the meat and places it in the pan. "Next?"

Leah repeats the step.

Looking around, I realize scrambled eggs wait on our plates, probably growing cold. Okay, so he doesn't multi-task very well, but he definitely is learning on the job. Watching him, I fall even more in love with him than I already am.

It feels strange, seeing the two of them in my kitchen, doing a routine I normally enjoy with my daughter. I am not going to be needed all the time anymore, and that's hard to accept. But it also brings me great joy.

"Can I wake Mommy now?" Leah asks.

I'm not so easily forgotten, I think with a grin. "I'm right here." I walk into the room and meet Nick's gaze. Everything from last night passes between us with that one searing look.

I clear my throat.

"Mommy! We're making eggs n' bacon. And I poured my own orange juice!" Leah, still in her pajamas, jumps up and down excitedly, as Nick turns back to the stove to concentrate on the frying pan.

We sit together as a family and eat breakfast, and I don't think I'll ever forget this first time. My heart is full, and I am…happy in a way I've never been before.

"You promised me Unicorn Poo!" Leah says.

I grin. "I did."

Leah sneezes and wipes her nose on her sleeve.

"Gross, young lady. Use a tissue," I say, not meeting Nick's gaze because I can see how badly he wants to laugh. "Go get some tissues from the bathroom."

Leah slides off her chair and runs to do as she's been asked. She sneezes again on her way there and again on her way back.

She returns with the entire box of tissues.

"Are you feeling okay?" I put my hand against Leah's forehead, finding it hot.

"My throat feels funny." Leah lets out an exaggerated cough.

This time, it's Nick who says, "Cover your mouth when you cough."

I shoot him a grateful look. "Since you two made us such a good breakfast, how about I clean up? You can watch something until I'm finished. Then I'll run your bath."

"Okay, Mommy."

I glance at Leah, noticing her eyes are a little glassy. "Can you get Mommy the thermometer from where we keep it?"

Leah runs out of the room.

"You think she's sick?" Nick asks, his face etched with concern.

"Looks like she may be coming down with something. It's probably a cold. I'll see how things go the rest of today."

Leah returns at the same time Nick's cell rings. He picks it up from the counter and takes the call.

"Here." Leah hands me the thermometer and brushes her hair away from her ear, waiting for her temperature to be taken.

"What? Jesus. Not again," Nick says, obviously exasperated.

I glance over. He is running his hand through his hair as he paces the length of the kitchen. In the end, he steps out of the room.

I put the thermometer in Leah's ear and wait for the beep before checking it. "Ninety-nine. There's definitely something brewing. Okay, monkey. I'm going to give you some Tylenol, a short bath, and we're going to rest today. How does a movie sound?"

"Good." Leah's normal enthusiasm is waning. She doesn't even ask for a movie with a prince.

Nick walks back into the room, tension radiating from his stiff body and annoyed expression.

"What's wrong?"

"You first. How is she?" he asks.

Leah walks over and throws herself against his legs in dramatic fashion. "I have a fever."

I laugh and roll my eyes. "Leah, go get your stuff ready for your bath. Don't forget pajamas and underwear this time." I ruffle my daughter's hair, and Leah drags herself out of the room.

"Is it just a cold?" Nick asks, his concern obvious.

I nod. "The fever is low grade. A little Children's Tylenol will help. As long as it doesn't turn into croup, we're good."

"Croup?"

"That's when they get a cough that sounds more like a bark."

Nick nods. "I think my younger brothers have had it before."

"She's had it a few times already. It's more of a winter illness and the doctor says she should outgrow it soon. But you never know. Occasionally it can happen in spring, though that's more unusual." Thinking back to those past episodes, I cringe. "The noise she makes with every cough is scary as hell. It's like a bark from her chest." I place my hands over my sternum. "When she was a baby, I had nights where I'd sit up in the rocker in her room because I felt better knowing I was there as she slept."

"Jesus." He runs a hand through his hair, an obvious habit when he's stressed. "I really wish I'd been with you then."

"It's fine, Nick. You're here now. I'll give her a fast bath, and she can relax for the day." I glance at the phone clenched in his hand. I've forgotten about his call. "Is everything okay?" I point to the cell.

He frowns. "It's the Miami hotel. We had a major flood and had to shut down the dining room. I need to go down there and handle things."

Disappointment rushes through me, but I push it away. "No problem."

It isn't like Nick lives with us. I don't expect him

to be around all the time. Besides, this is his job—even though his comings and goings bring out the worst of my insecurities.

Whatever our relationship is, I need to get a hold of myself, and not immediately equate his traveling with abandonment.

If only it can be that easy.

★   ★   ★

Nick

ALTHOUGH I NEED to leave, I push work aside and stay, giving myself another hour with my girls. Leah seems to wilt as time goes on. She didn't even ask for the Unicorn Poo in her bath, which tells me how badly she's feeling. Aurora knows enough not to bring up Zach's gift, obviously sensing Leah is too tired to notice.

And that reminds me how much I still have to learn.

I sit through some of *Cinderella*, Leah's head in Aurora's lap, watching them more than the movie, until the little girl falls asleep. I nod at Aurora, and she slides out from beneath our daughter, leaving her conked out on the sofa.

Aurora walks me to the door.

"Do you promise she's okay? I can go without worrying?" I ask.

She nods. "She's sleeping and barely coughing. I'll see how she does overnight. Maybe I'll keep her home from school tomorrow. And if she starts that bark, I'll make an appointment with the pediatrician. Sometimes they give her steroids to reduce the swelling in her airways."

I flinch at the description. "Maybe I should stay." Of course, then no one will be available for the Florida debacle.

Aurora sounds calm and confident. She's definitely pulled back since last night, but I'll just have to see how she handles me being away again.

"What about you? Are *you* okay?" I ask.

Aurora treats me to a practiced smile. "I've handled Leah being sick before. No worries," she says too easily.

"Yes, you have. But you're not alone anymore. I'm here, too." I reach for her hands and hold them tight, needing her to feel our connection. To remember what we shared last night.

"And Leah's lucky to have you," she says.

My gut starts churning. "I'm also here for you," I remind her. And I'll keep reminding her until she believes me. "You'll keep in touch?"

She nods. "Of course. I'll let you know how she's doing."

I do my best not to grind my teeth at her obvious withdrawal. "I'll check in at the usual times." We've come up with a routine during my travels, and I know how much Aurora likes her schedules.

"Thank you. That's great. What time are you leaving?"

She tugs her hands, and I release her. "As soon as I pack and get to Teterboro Airport." Where the company jet hangar is located.

"Okay, well, fly safe," she says, as she opens the door.

I've had enough of this bullshit. I wraps my hands around her waist and pull her against me. "Goodbye, Aurora. I'll be back," I say, then leave her with a long, deep kiss to keep with her while I'm gone.

Finally, I turn and walk away, heading to my car.

The sooner I leave, the sooner I'll return.

Aurora

NICK HAS JUST left when Leah wakes up. And now, I have no doubt that my daughter is sick. It is as if a switch has been turned on. Leah's gone from being slightly feverish, to having a full-blown cold with a cough that makes me nervous. I do my best to keep

Leah calm, because I've learned that panic and anxiety will only make the cough worse.

From *Cinderella* to *Frozen* to *Beauty and the Beast*, we watch Disney princesses all day and into the night. The first night is manageable, and we speak to Nick as planned. I'm too worried about the rumble in Leah's chest to focus on Nick's absence, which I suppose is a good thing.

When Leah wakes up in the morning, she still has a fever and a cough, but she seems calmer, and the cough is under control. I call school and explain Leah won't be in and once again, we watch movies or I read her stories. When she naps, I check in at work, but Billie has things under control.

Nick calls while we're eating breakfast, and I have Leah answer, to assure him she's okay. Or so I tell myself, knowing I don't buy my own bullshit. I'm keeping Nick at a distance for my own emotional safety again. The man told me he loves me. What more do I need?

"Mommy, I'm hungry," Leah says, followed by a barking cough that I know isn't good.

"Let's go into your room so you're close to the humidifier, and I'll make you some chicken soup for dinner." I kiss Leah's forehead. Still warm. She's due for more Tylenol after she eats. It is only four o'clock, but I'll feed Leah twice if need be.

After setting up Leah in her room with a picture book and a stuffed animal, I walk into the kitchen. While I heat the soup, I call the doctor's office, and we talk about the usual remedies. The nurse says they will fit Leah in tomorrow if the fever doesn't break or her cough gets any worse.

After dinner, I give Leah more Tylenol and field calls from Nick. One thing I can say about Nick—he obviously loves his daughter, if all his calls checking in on her are any indication. I downplay how bad Leah's cough and fever are because as frustrated as I am by Nick being away, I don't want him to worry when there is nothing he can do from where he is.

I spend the early part of the evening bringing Leah in and out of the steam-filled shower and my heart breaks with every whine, bark-like cough, and cry.

I pray we'll soon turn a corner, but later that night, Leah's cough morphs into something that terrifies me. Her breathing isn't strong, even when she isn't coughing, and high-pitched wheezes come from her chest. Then Leah panics and starts to cry, which sets off more coughing.

Around ten, Leah is having trouble breathing, and I know I have to take her to the hospital. I call Melly, but she doesn't answer her phone. Everyone else is too far away. So I'm left with two choices—either call for an ambulance, or take Leah to the hospital myself.

With no desire to traumatize Leah even more, I decide to drive.

I walk over to Leah, who has glassy eyes and a red, runny nose. She looks miserable and when she coughs harder, she starts to cry. "Mommy, it hurts." She presses her hands to her chest, the tears breaking my heart.

"I know, baby. We're going to go see the doctor." I don't say hospital. No need to scare her.

I bundle her up against the cool spring air and walk into the garage. When I open the door for Leah to get in, my normally easygoing daughter shakes her head.

"What's wrong?"

"I don't want to be alone in the back." She folds her arms and leans against the wall, refusing to move. Then, as if on cue, she begins to cough and cry.

I close my eyes and try not to cry myself. I reached into my bag and call Mark. He is next door, and I am out of options.

Once Mark hears Leah's cough, he puts aside any lingering hard feelings and goes into action. I call Samantha, who rushes over to stay with a sleeping Mimi, and as soon as she arrives, Mark pulls his car into my driveaway.

The hospital isn't far, though with Leah crying, barking and wheezing, I feel every moment. My priority is to get Leah settled and then I'll call Nick.

Mark drops me at the ER while he goes to find a parking spot. Normally, there would be a check-in and triage, but the woman behind the desk is kind and realizes Leah can't breathe well.

They rush Leah and me into a private cubicle and a nurse comes in. Together, we calm Leah down and a female doctor arrives a few minutes later.

"Relax, honey." I hold Leah's hand so the doctor can listen to her chest. Leah has been through this many times before at the pediatrician's office, so she isn't scared and lets the doctor check her over.

"I want to get x-rays taken," the doctor says. "We have a mobile machine so I'll have someone from imaging and radiology come up. In the meantime, let's get a nebulizer treatment going." She hooks her stethoscope around her neck. "We're also going to give her IV steroids." She smiles at Leah. "I'm going to need you to be a big girl for this, but you're going to feel better quickly."

The woman tips her head towards the door, and I nod. Before I can tell Leah I'll be right outside, Mark joins us.

"I told them I was her father," he says to me, as he hurries inside.

I stare at him, surprised. I don't like it, but I know he cares, and it's the only way he could get back here to check what's going on.

I step away from him and stride to the bed, running my hand over Leah's hair. "I'm going to talk to the nice doctor. Mark will stay with you, and you'll be able to see me right outside the door, okay?"

Leah opens her mouth to answer, and a loud barking sound comes out instead. Tears form in her eyes, and it is all I can do to hold back my own. I wish Nick was here, but he's in Florida and I am alone. So I nod at the doctor and follow her outside.

"I'm going to keep her overnight so I can give her IV fluids," the doctor says. "It's normal for children to get dehydrated when they can't eat or drink without coughing. We'll monitor her oxygen levels and get some steroids going in the IV."

I manage a nod. "She's had croup before, just never like this."

"She'll be fine." The doctor, whose name tag says Dr. Fleischer, gives me a reassuring smile. "We just want to help speed things along and make her more comfortable."

"Thank you, Dr. Fleischer." The tag is helpful. I would never remember it on my own. "I can stay with her, right?" The thought of leaving my baby alone is enough to give me a panic attack.

"Of course. Our pediatric ward is set up for parents."

"Thank you." I walk back into the room, pasting

on a happy smile for Leah's sake. "We're going to stay tonight," I say. "How about that for an adventure?"

Leah nods, obviously having decided to stop trying to speak. Dammit. My heart squeezes in my chest.

I turn to my neighbor. "Mark, thank you so much for getting us here. I didn't want to traumatize Leah more with an ambulance ride."

"I'm here for you both," he says, reaching out a hand to touch my shoulder.

"Thank you. But why don't you go home now? Mimi will be scared if she wakes up and you're not there. I'm going to text my family and let them know what's going on." And Nick. I planned to call him, but then I decided to wait until I knew more. I probably missed his late-night call, and I haven't checked my phone at all. I've been focused on Leah. I'm going to have to get better about remembering I'm was now part of a team where Leah is concerned. I've been a single parent so long, I'm having trouble adjusting.

It takes a few more minutes to convince Mark to leave, and I admit to myself I'm relieved when he's gone.

Then I turn my attention to my daughter. A nurse speaks gently to her as she opens everything needed to put an IV into Leah's arm. I stand by the edge of the bed and hold Leah's legs—the only part of her I can reach—and prepare myself for a long night.

Once the ordeal with the needle is over with, I call Nick.

Nick

I FINISH DINNER with the manager for the Meridian Miami. I poached the man from another five-star hotel a couple of years ago, and he's been a great addition. Thomas Breckenridge wanted to work for a family-owned company with smaller boutique hotels, has twenty years of experience, and the employees respond to him. After the long couple of days we've had overseeing the flood and dealing with contractors and upset customers, I feel obligated to take the man to dinner.

I've just signed the bill and shaken Breckenridge's hand when my phone rings. The other man walks away, and I reached into my pocket for my cell.

Aurora's name shows up on the screen. I tried to call her before dinner, but nobody picked up. I assume she had Leah in the bath.

"Nick?"

"Hey. It's good to hear your voice." I stride across the lobby, towards the elevators, where there are less people and noise. "What's going on? How's Leah feeling?" I've struggled being away while she's sick. Talking to her on Facetime, seeing her little red nose and sad expression, hits me hard.

"Umm, don't panic, but her cough got bad, her chest hurt, and she had trouble catching her breath. I took her to the hospital," Aurora says.

"Shit. Is she okay?" I begin to pace the lobby, one hand on the phone, the other running through my hair.

"She is. They're keeping her overnight as a precaution but she's going to be fine." Aurora sounds exhausted and worried.

And I'm a good two and a half, no three-hour flight away, as well as the time it would take me to get to the hospital. "Are you sure you're not holding anything back because I'm not there?" I ask.

Her sigh echoes in my ear. "I swear, Nick. They've got her on a saline nebulizer treatment and put in an IV for steroids once they move her to a room."

IV? They're sticking a needle in my kid's arm, and I was eating a steak dinner. Fuck. "Okay," I say, forcing myself to remain calm, at least to Aurora. Inside, my stomach is churning because I need to be there.

I finally force myself to walk to the nearest window overlooking the street and stop pacing.

"How is everything at the hotel?" she asks.

"Fine. I handled all I could. The manager will take

over from there. I'll be on an eleven a.m. flight tomorrow."

Her silence speaks volumes about how she's feeling about my trip. "Look, I'd take the jet home now, but Asher needed it and it's no longer in Miami." There won't be a normal flight this late, so I'll have to travel on the one I've already booked.

"I understand," she says.

I hope so. "Can I talk to Leah?"

"I'm sorry. She's asleep," Aurora says.

Disappointment hits me hard. "Hey, what about you? How are you holding up?"

"I'm running on adrenaline. There's a couch in her room and I can stretch out there, but I doubt I'll sleep. I'm just glad they let me stay over."

I lean against the tempered glass. "Me, too."

"Yes, come on in," she says. "Nick? The nurse just came in to check Leah's vitals. I need to go."

"Okay. I hate that I'm not there with you, but I'm a phone call away if you need anything." And I'll get home as soon as possible.

I hang up, emptiness and frustration consuming me. Then I walk into the elevator and up to my room. I want to be with Aurora so she knows she isn't alone. Dammit. I wish I listened to my gut and stayed home.

And there it is. The man who has no permanent address now thinks of Aurora's house in New York as home.

CHAPTER TEN

Aurora

I OPEN MY eyes and immediately look over at Leah. She is still propped up on pillows, asleep. Between the nebulizer saline treatments and the steroids in the IV, they calmed the spasms in her airways and eased her cough. I have no doubt those same steroids will have her hopped up and anxious later, but I'll worry about one thing at a time.

I sit up and discover I have a crick in my neck from sleeping on the small couch. I stand, stretching my back and rolling my head from side to side. I'll have to ask a nurse for ibuprofen to ease the discomfort, but first I need a cup of coffee to get myself moving.

I walk to the bathroom located in Leah's private room and do my best to clean myself up with the small toiletry bag the hospital provides. I don't want to go all the way to the cafeteria and leave Leah alone. Luckily, after talking to the morning nurse, the lovely woman brings me a cup of coffee.

Leah wakes up and is fussy this morning, but I

don't blame her. Everything hurts, from the coughing to the IV, and she was awakened during the night to have her vitals taken. Even I'm cranky, though a second cup of coffee is helping.

I stand by Leah's bed, sipping my drink, when a knock sounds on the door. Expecting a nurse, I look up to see Mark walk in.

"Hi, Mr. Wheeler," Leah says.

"Hi, Leah. How are you feeling this morning?" he asks.

She puts on her best pouty face. "I don't feel good."

Mark nods in understanding. "I bet you don't. Mimi said to say hi," he tells her.

"I miss Mimi."

"You'll see her soon," I say. I pick up the TV remote and turn on a show for Leah, then glance at Mark and tip my head, indicating I want to talk.

I walk a few steps into the hall and turn to face him. "I really appreciate your help last night, but you didn't need to drive all the way back here."

"I wanted to see how you both were doing," he says, putting a hand on my shoulder.

I nod, and decide against telling him he could have called or sent a text. I don't want to be rude, and after all, we are neighbors. I want to keep things positive between us. After all, I definitely needed his help last night. "That was kind of you. We're fine, as you can see."

I glance over at Leah who is immersed in television, fascinated by how the voice comes out over the remote control. "How did you get up here? Hospital policy is family only."

He shoots me a sheepish grin. "Just like last night, I told them I was her father."

"I'm sorry, *what?*"

Nick's sudden appearance takes me off guard. "Nick! You said your flight wasn't until later this morning."

Nick appears as exhausted as I feel. He wears a pair of jeans and a wrinkled t-shirt, but he still looks extremely hot, with the scruff on his handsome face and his dark hair messy from what had to be his hands running through it.

Then again, whether he has slicked hair or messy strands, the man looks sexy. While he's been gone, when I wasn't worried about Leah, I've been thinking about my last night with Nick. My body was putty in his hands. I never felt a sense of belonging before, the way I did when we came together. And when I see him standing in the doorway, here and not in Florida, I feel better than I have in days. I'm not alone.

I don't know how to have a relationship—or believe in them, really. But if I'm going to try for anyone, it will be Nick. Will he have patience for my issues? I don't even trust my own family to show up this morning. I rarely verbalize my feelings, but I can sum them up in one sentence—it is better to push people away before they disappoint me.

Nick looks from Mark to me. "I hired a private plane and figured I'd surprise you. I certainly didn't expect to see another man playing daddy." He turns to scowl at my neighbor.

To his credit, Mark's face flushes red. "I was just trying to be helpful. Aurora called me last night and asked me to drive them to the hospital. It was the only way they'd let me up so I could check on them. I didn't want Aurora to be alone."

Oh, God. This might go south fast, I think. "Nick—"

He shakes his head and glances at her neighbor. "Mark, I appreciate you being here for my girls when I couldn't be." He extends his hand, taking me off-guard.

And Mark, too, if his stunned expression is anything to go by. Mark accepts Nick's hand. He looks between us, obviously gauging the tension in the room and trying to figure out what his role is.

"Aurora, I'm glad Leah's okay. If you run into trouble, you know I'm right next door," Mark says, taking the hint. "Nick." He tips his head and leaves, heading out into the hall.

"Well, that was awkward," Nick mutters.

I bite my bottom lip with my teeth and release it. "I had no choice. In any of it," I say, hating how defensive I sound. "I brought Leah to the car and she refused to get in the backseat alone. So I called Mark to take us."

"And assume the role of her father?"

"That was his idea. He wanted to get past the desk and check on what was going on. I had no idea he would show up again this morning." I look up at Nick, so grateful he's here. "That was very magnanimous of you, the way you handled Mark at the end."

Nick shrugs. "I might not appreciate how he acts but you're right. He was here when I wasn't. I can't exactly complain when he helped you out."

But the pain he feels at hearing someone else calling himself Leah's daddy is obvious, and I melt towards him. Ignoring the voice in my head that is always there, the one reminding me to protect myself, I run to him and he catches me, wrapping his arms around me and pulling me close.

Nick

I MANAGED TO make some calls and rent a private jet, enabling me to leave earlier this morning. And now that Aurora is in my arms, I know I've done the right thing. Her body shakes against mine, and I realize she is finally letting go of her fear and pain, all the emotions she's had to hold in.

I stroke her silky hair with my hand, giving her what comfort I can. "How is she?" I ask.

Aurora releases me and steps back. Her eyes are red, and dark circles have formed beneath them, but she is still the most beautiful woman I've ever seen.

"They're giving her steroids and nebulizer treatments. Both have calmed things down enough for her to sleep. She's exhausted from having that awful cough."

"I'm sure you're wiped out, too. Where is your family?" I ask, surprised she isn't surrounded by her siblings.

"I tried to reach Melly last night. I wanted to ask her to go with me to the hospital, but there was no answer. She called this morning when she got my message, and I told her not to rush over. The doctor said they'd send Leah home later today. Besides, visiting hours don't start until noon."

"And the rest of the family?" I'm pushing her on

purpose. She's been here all night, alone, and I want to know why.

"I didn't want to bother them. They all live so far away. It would take a long time for any of them to get here. Leah and I were fine," she insists.

I narrow my gaze. Does she not realize how she's deliberately sabotaged the very things she craves?

"Mommy?" Leah's raspy, low voice calls out from inside the room, followed by coughing that hurts me to hear.

If this is sounding better, I can't imagine what Aurora has been dealing with.

Aurora meets my gaze, and I follow her into the room.

"Hey, baby!" Aurora rushes over and eases herself down on the bed. "Look who's here."

Before I even make it to her other side, Leah's eyes light up. "*Daddy!*" Her exclamation results in a coughing fit that has me wincing.

But I can't miss the joy that fills me at what Leah called me. I look at Aurora, wondering how she'll take the change, but all I see is a soft smile on her lips.

"Yeah, baby. I'm here," I say, with a lump in the back of my throat. I walk around to the head of the bed, pushing the IV pole out of the way.

Tears from coughing track down Leah's little face and she swipes at them with the back of her free hand.

The other arm has the I.V. in.

"How are you feeling this morning?" Aurora asks softly.

Leah rubs her eyes, her skin still pale. "My arm hurts." She points to the tape holding the IV needle where her arm bends.

"I'm sure they'll take it out soon," Aurora reassures her.

"My throat hurts, too."

I slide my hand over her head, then lean down and kiss her cheek.

"That's from coughing," Aurora says. "Let me go talk to the nurse. Maybe they can get you something to drink, okay?"

Leah bobs her head.

"Nick...I mean, Daddy will stay with you." Aurora rises to her feet and rushes out to find a nurse.

"Hey, kid. I missed you," I say.

Eyes so like my own look back at him. "I missed you, too. Me and Mommy watched sooo many movies," she says in the dramatic fashion I adore.

I chuckle. "I bet you did."

"Here you go. Apple juice." Aurora comes back into the room and hands her a plastic cup with the sealed foil top pulled back and a straw inside. "I'll hold it. You sip."

Leah slurps down a good amount of the drink,

which I'm pleased to see.

"Ms. Kingston?" A nurse steps inside.

"Yes?"

The redheaded nurse smiles. "The main desk called up. You have family downstairs, and there are too many people to let up at once."

Aurora blinks, her eyes wide in obvious surprise. "Oh! I'll go down and talk to them. Is it okay if we do shifts, so a couple of people can see her? Or would it be better if I ask them to go to Leah's grandmother's place, where they can see Leah later," she says, more to herself than to the nurse.

"I think that second option might work better," the woman says.

I withhold my grin. Of course, her family has shown up, despite her telling them not to come. She has a lot to learn about what families do for those they love. And I intend to teach her.

We haven't had another conversation about our feelings or the future, but I have to be optimistic. Without hope, what else is there?

Nick

I INSIST ON going down and handling her family so

that Aurora can stay with Leah. I step out of the elevator on the lobby floor, walk down the hall, and turn the corner to the front reception area of the hospital. I spot Aurora's family immediately, congregated in a small group. There aren't as many Kingstons here as I thought. Still, they feel like an army, much like my family.

I glance around, looking for someone I recognize from Leah's birthday party. Melly catches my gaze first.

"Nick!" Melly rushes over and surprises me by greeting me with a warm hug. "Is Leah okay?" she asks, stepping back. "I feel so guilty! I fell asleep early and left my phone in another room so I missed Aurora's call."

"She's better, or so Aurora tells me. The cough still sounds pretty scary." I shudder just thinking of the sound coming from Leah's little chest.

Melly nods. "Croup can test any parent, as you'll learn." She pats my arm.

"Who else is here?" I ask.

"Linc came but Jordan had to go see her mother. Chloe and Beck said they'd call Aurora tonight. Xander and Sasha are over there." She gestures to the corner where Sasha, wearing a baseball cap low on her eyes, does her best not to be noticed.

Somehow, she's been managing to live a normal

life, and according to Harrison, she is happier than she's ever been. "And of course, Dash and Cassidy are home with the baby."

"Makes sense. The front desk didn't want to let more than two people up at one time, so I offered to come down and give you all an update." I smile at Melly. "Why don't I give you my pass, for starters. Tell them you're going up, and we'll switch when you're done."

Melly's eyes light up. "I just want to see Leah for myself. I won't stay long."

"Can we talk, first?" I didn't plan to have a personal conversation, but I feel compelled to talk to this woman who's become my daughter's grandmother, despite the circumstances.

"Of course." Melly grasps my arm and leads me to a private corner near a large, marble pillar. "What is it? Is Aurora all right?" Her concern is obvious in the tiny wrinkles beside her eyes.

And that is why I want to speak with her. "Aurora is tired but fine." I draw a deep breath. "I just wanted to say thank you."

"For what?" Melly is an attractive woman with dark, shoulder-length hair. Her makeup is flawless, but she is anything but the ice queen her look might imply.

"For being there when I couldn't. For taking Aurora in and giving her a home," I say. While I was partying in college, Aurora was alone until Linc found her. "It takes a special human being to take in her husband's illegitimate, pregnant daughter," I say. "And I'm not trying to flatter you to win you over. I mean it."

Melly links her hands together and meets my gaze. "I knew my husband wasn't a saint. But I did not know he was capable of turning his back on his own child." She draws a deep breath. "By the time Linc discovered Aurora, she was alone and pregnant. I didn't see her as my husband's illegitimate child. I saw her as a young girl all alone in the world, about to give birth."

My stomach turns over. Despite already knowing the details, they hurt to hear. "All the more reason for me to stand by my statement. You're a special person." And because I have a stepmom with an equally big heart, I know what I'm talking about.

"Thank you," Melly murmurs, her eyes suspiciously damp. "Now let's talk about you. I know you didn't abandon Aurora. It was an unfortunate set of circumstances."

I nod.

"But you're here now and I'm putting my faith in you. You owe me nothing, but you owe *them* everything," she says, patting my shoulder.

I am aware. "Those abandonment issues she has…

I can never tell when I'm making any progress. I'll think we've come to an understanding, then something will happen…" Like an emergency phone call that takes me away. "And she retreats."

"And that's where your tenacity will have to come in," Melly says with an assured grin.

Linc walks over and kisses his mother's cheek. "Are you giving Nick a hard time? I thought that was my job." His grin tells me he is only partially joking.

"Lincoln, behave!"

I chuckle at Melly's scolding. That works better than any comeback I might have.

Ignoring Aurora's overprotective brother, I meet Melly's gaze. "What you just said to me? You're right. And I will do whatever I can to make up for the time I missed."

Financially and emotionally, I think. But I don't intend to tell anyone but Aurora just how I intend to do that.

Melly smiles. "Good. Now I'm going up to see Aurora and Leah. Thank you, Nick."

"My pleasure."

"Weren't you supposed to be in Florida?" Linc asks.

I narrow my gaze. "I flew in this morning."

"Aurora called you?" Linc sounds surprised.

I nod. "I take it she didn't contact you?"

Linc shoves his hands into his front pockets of his slacks. "No. My mother let us all know. To be honest, I'm surprised she texted Mom, let alone you. It must mean you've made progress with those walls of hers."

"I'm trying," I admit. "Aurora told me that she asked Melly not to come to the hospital."

Linc groans. "Frustrating woman," he mutters. "As if that would keep us away." A few seconds tick by in silence until Linc speaks again. "You seem to know Aurora pretty well for a man who hasn't seen her in years."

I refrain from rolling my eyes at the other man's attempt at a dig. I understand Linc's protectiveness. Admire it, even.

"All Aurora had to do was tell me her history. From there, it wasn't difficult to figure out the way she thinks." That, and I've made it my mission to understand her so I can learn how to reassure her, and ultimately, win her over.

"Yeah. Her parents really fucked with her head. Or should I say, the fact that they weren't in her life did. I wish I'd never had to tell her the truth."

I lean against the pillar. "The truth always comes out. Now that she knows, she can begin to put it behind her." I shrug. "Assuming she learns she can trust the people who love her."

"And do you? Love her, I mean?" Linc asks.

"Do you really think that's any of your business?" But I take pity on the guy. "Aurora is all I can think about. She's the only woman I've ever considered having a future with. We just…click."

Linc taps his feet on the floor. "I screwed up things with Jordan badly. She was in my life for years and I was blind to what she meant to me. Let's hope Aurora didn't inherit those stubborn genes."

I hope for the same thing.

★   ★   ★

Aurora

I SIT ON the small couch in Leah's hospital room while Melly reads to my daughter from a short book she brought with her. I'm grateful. Melly's presence distracts Leah from thinking about her ordeal, and that distraction gives me a much-needed break. I can sit and breathe for a few minutes. Of course, my thoughts are on Nick, who is downstairs with my family, which makes me wonder if that ought to make me nervous.

Melly sits down beside me and sighs. "Poor baby. She's so exhausted."

We glance at Leah, who has fallen asleep, wheezy noises still coming from her chest. Thank God they aren't as bad they were last night.

Carly Phillips

"You need to get some rest, too," Melly says, running a hand over my tangled hair in that motherly fashion that I recognize. I do the same thing with Leah, even though I never experienced it as a child.

"Once we get home, I'll sleep when she does," I say.

"Or you can let Nick come home with you and look after Leah while you take care of yourself. You won't be any good to that child if you crash and burn." Melly's Chanel flats tap against the hospital floor.

I bite down on the inside of my cheek. "I could, but I don't want to put him out. He's been traveling and working hard for the last couple of days—"

Melly puts her hand up, stopping me midsentence. "Are you trying to make that man so exasperated he walks away?"

I blink. "What? No? I'm just telling you the truth."

"Are you? Or are you being a martyr, doing everything yourself, so you don't have to risk your heart?"

This is as blunt as Melly has ever been with me, and I turn to face her in shock. "Why would you say that? I'm not a martyr."

Melly takes my hands in hers. "Can we agree that I'm the closest thing to a mother that you've ever had?"

Tears fill my eyes as I nod.

"Then listen to me. I married a man I loved and he

228

cheated on me. Repeatedly. Instead of divorcing him, I opted to keep my family together and ignore what he did behind my back."

Even though Kenneth Kingston was my father, Melly has never spoken of him before. Not even when she graciously took me—a pregnant stranger—into her home. I just moved in and we formed our own relationship. If it was odd that he was some sort of background spectre in our lives, gone but hovering between us, I never let herself think about him. My heart pounds hard and my mouth grows dry as I wait for Melly to continue.

"When Linc told me about you, I was horrified that Kenneth had abandoned you. And when I discovered what your mother had done? I was furious on your behalf. I took you in because you deserved to have the opportunity to have a good life. What do you think others thought?" Melly asks.

I look around the hospital room, at the painted flowers on the bland walls, anywhere but at Melly. "You took your husband's mistress's pregnant daughter into your home. I'm sure they thought you'd lost your mind." Some said as much.

I recall the baby shower Melly threw for me and the cruel words I overheard from some of Melly's *friends* about the *bastard child* having her own bastard.

I shudder at the memory. I was new to town, new

to the family and felt so out of place. But I was so grateful, I never said a word about it to Melly. The woman did way too much for me to ever complain or hurt her. But I realize that Melly's inner circle has grown smaller over the past couple of years.

"Aurora, look at me."

I turn to meet Melly's gaze and focus on the hands that now squeeze mine tighter.

"No matter what they said—and I was aware people would talk, by the way—I knew I'd be getting so much more out of my choice than they could understand. I got you, who I consider another daughter, and my first grandchild."

"Oh, Melly." I throw my arms around her and hug her tight. The other woman reciprocates. "I love you and I'm so grateful," I say, telling my mother-by-chance the words for the first time.

"Honey, I love you too." She pats my back before pulling away so she can meet my gaze. "Don't you see? I had to put myself out there and trust that you weren't a con artist or someone out to take advantage of my family. I heard about you and I just knew you were supposed to be ours. You belong with us—with our whole big, nutty family." Melly's eyes are glassy, her smile sweet.

"I can't imagine what would have happened to me without you. Without all of you." Of course, the

Prescotts were kind to me, but they weren't my family.

"What I'm getting at—and I know I'm taking the long way to make my point—is can you imagine your life, your future, without Nick in it? If he came around to be Leah's daddy, but not the man in your life? All because you can't move past the fact that the people in your past let you down?"

Big fat tears drip from my eyes, and I hold back a sob.

Melly wraps an arm around me and hugs me tight. "You've been strong for so long because you've had to be. But you're not alone anymore. You have a huge family who loves you, and a man downstairs, who's doing his best to prove that he does too."

I sniff, wiping my damp face with my sleeve. I laugh at myself and rise to grab the tissues by a sink before I sit back down. "Nick travels a lot. Every time he leaves, I'm overcome with that lost, abandoned feeling I hate. It makes me feel weak and needy," I admit.

Melly places a hand beneath my chin. "You're none of those things. You need to see reality through a new lens—not through the past. Nick travels, yes, but he always comes back. It's up to you whether or not you can open your heart and take the risk." She removes her hand. "Now I'm going to leave so that handsome man can come back up. I'll take the family home with me. Give us a ring when you and Leah are up to visitors, once you're back home again." She gathers her purse and starts for the door.

"Melly?"

She turns back, hand on the doorframe. "Yes?"

"Thank you. For everything."

Melly smiles and blows a kiss. Then she's gone.

I stand for a while, staring at nothing, thinking about the things Melly said. We never broached such sensitive, difficult subjects before, but our talk was long overdue. And Melly made good points about whether or not I can give up a relationship with Nick just to protect my heart. Can I imagine a future with Nick as Leah's father and nothing more?

With a sigh, I walk over to Leah and stand by her bed, watching my daughter sleep. She is so sweet and innocent, and she'll grow up surrounded by love. No matter what issues she might have—because everyone has some—abandonment will never be one of them.

I lean down and kiss Leah's forehead. "I love you, and I'll always be here."

"So will I, if you let me."

I spin around at the sound of Nick's voice. He steps into the room and joins me at the bed.

"Is everything okay?" he asks, coming up beside me and placing his big hand on my back.

I look into his familiar bedroom eyes and everything I feel comes rushing at me with the force of a tidal wave.

This is it. The moment I have to decide if I'm going to run from that wave…or ride it. "Nick," I whisper.

"What is it?"

I reach for him when someone knocks.

"Guess who's going home today?" the nurse calls out in a loud, sing-song voice, walking in and waving papers.

Leah pops up from her bed and rubs her eyes. "I can go home?"

The nurse smiles. "Yes. As soon as your mom signs these papers and I take out the IV."

Nick glances at me. "Whatever you were about to say? I want to hear."

I swallow hard and manage a nod. I wish the woman hadn't interrupted. I could have told him how I feel, and what I want. Now I have to wait, nervous and ready to jump out of my skin, until the next time Nick and I are alone.

CHAPTER ELEVEN

Nick

I TAKE AURORA and Leah home from the hospital in the car I rented at the airport. I know it's too much to hope my little chatterbox will fall back asleep so her mother and I can have a serious conversation. Instead, we talk about Leah's adventures at the hospital, her sore throat, and the fact that her arm still hurts from the IV needle. I have a feeling she'll be milking that one for weeks.

Aurora remembers she has a lollipop in her bag and hands it to Leah, which keeps her quiet for a few minutes.

Then she leans closer to me. Her lingering vanilla scent tortures me and my cock jerks like fucking Pavlov's dog. After our night together, I don't think I've ever not gotten hard at the intoxicating smell.

"I was impressed with how you handled Mark this morning," she says quietly, so little ears won't hear.

I stiffen at the surprise topic. "I know he lives next door. It would have been stupid for me to start an argument with him, even though it gutted me that he was here when I wasn't."

Admitting the truth isn't easy, because Aurora doesn't like my trips and she doesn't need a reminder of them. But I'm Leah's father. I should have been around.

"I know," she says. "And I also realize how much it took for you to accept what he did and thank him. I appreciate it.'

"That doesn't mean I didn't want to punch him," I mutter.

She lets out a surprised laugh, causing me to grin.

"What's funny?" Leah yells from the backseat, and of course, starts to cough.

"I need to buy an SUV with the screens in the headrest," I say to Aurora. "Nothing, Leah. Just grown-up stuff."

"I hate grown up stuff."

I glance in the rearview mirror in time to see her stick the lollipop back in her mouth. My lips twitch and a quick side glance tells him Aurora is holding back a chuckle, too.

No sooner do we arrive home before Leah announces she's starving. I take one look at Aurora and make an executive decision.

"I'm going to make you something to eat. Your mommy is going to take a nap and then have a long, hot shower. Or a long hot, shower and then a nap.

Whatever she needs." I meet Aurora's gaze and she treats me to the most appreciative smile I've ever seen, one that causes my heart to beat faster and makes me think that she just might be coming around. "How's that sound?" I ask Leah. But my gaze remains on Aurora's face.

"Can you make grilled cheese?" Leah asks.

"I can manage that."

"And tomato soup," she demands.

"No problem."

"With milk, not water."

I grin, and Aurora does, too.

She walks up to me, places her hands on either side of my face and pulls me in for a long kiss. No tongue, but I'll take it.

"Why are you kissing?" Leah asks, her face scrunched as she watches us.

Aurora grins. "Because Daddy just did a very nice thing for me. Now you be good for him, okay?"

Leah nods.

Aurora glances at me, gives me a smile I can't interpret, and heads to her room to take a much-needed nap, leaving me alone with my kid.

I make us lunch, we talk about her friends, their names, Leah's favorite color, animal and other things I want to know.

After we finish, I take a good look at my daughter.

She has orange tomato stains around her mouth, her hair sticks out every which way, and she needs a bath. But I'm not sure how to handle that challenge.

I pick up our dishes and take them to the sink, cleaning up as she watches. "Are you up to a bath or a shower?"

"Shower! I like showers. Mommy lets me come in with her sometimes, or I take one alone and she helps me rinse my hair."

I nod. "Daddy can help you clean up in the shower and your mom can give you a good washing tomorrow."

Her eyes light up, and she nods.

An hour later, I set Leah in front of the TV. I clean the water-soaked bathroom floor, which means I have to throw a load of soaking wet towels in the washing machine. But I take care of all the shit I can, so Aurora will be able to focus on Leah. Then I collapse on the couch beside my daughter.

I have a new respect for Aurora as a single mom and am more determined than ever to do right by her. My phone buzzes. I glance at the screen and answer the call. "Asher, how are you?" I ask my oldest sibling.

"I'm calling to find out how my niece is. Harrison told me Leah was in the hospital?" Asher asks.

Asher missed meeting Leah at our parents' house but that doesn't make him disinterested.

"It was a bad case of croup. It was scary as hell but it's under control now and she's home. At her mom's." I glance at Leah, happily sitting cross-legged beside me, watching something on her iPad, and ignoring the television I put on. Kids' music sounds so I'm not too worried. "Where are you?" I ask Asher.

"I got back from the island last night, and I visited with a friend this morning. I'm about half an hour from where you said Aurora lives. Mind if I drop by so I can meet Leah and Aurora?" My brother has a house on Windermere Island, near the Bahamas. It's connected to Eleuthera, private and secluded.

"Aurora's asleep. She was up most of the night at the hospital, but sure. Come on over. I'll text you the address."

I peeked in on Aurora earlier and she's out cold in her bed. She obviously needs the sleep, and I doubt she'll care if my brother visits.

About forty minutes later, I let Asher into the house. He has a big box in his hand. "Jesus, what did you do?"

"Asked my secretary what a five-year-old girl would want. Someone needs to be the cool uncle." He grins, and I roll my eyes.

"Zach bought her Unicorn Poo. Think you can beat that?" I lead him inside and introduce Leah to her Uncle Asher, who spends fifteen minutes talking to her, an amused smile on his face as he nods, not getting a word in edgewise.

When she opens her gift—an American Girl doll with blonde hair just like Leah—she jumps up and down with excitement. "Thank you!" she screeches, and I wince, putting a finger over my lips. "Indoor voice." I repeat what I've heard Aurora say, knowing she also needs to be kept calm after her stint in the hospital.

Leah holds her doll in her arms and nods.

Asher glances at me. "See? Cool uncle."

I feel a tug on my pants and glance at Leah. "What's up, princess?"

"I'm tired."

I pick her up and carried her to her room. "You've had quite the experience and nobody sleeps well in a hospital. How about you take a nap, like your mommy?" I ask, putting her down on the bed.

"I want to sleep with Mommy," she says.

I shrug. "Does she let you?"

"Duh!" She grabs her doll and runs out of the room.

I pad down the hall to Aurora's bedroom and glance in. Leah has already climbed beneath the covers and curls into her mother's arms. There isn't a sound from either one of them. I want to join them, but I have to console myself with, *maybe someday.*

I step out and return to the family room, dropping into the sofa beside Asher.

"You've got your hands full with that one," my brother says, but the smile on his face tells me he is as smitten with Leah as I am.

"No kidding." I stretch my legs out in front of me, lean my head back and groan. "But it's been a long fucking night and day." I could use some sleep myself. I raise my head and glance at Asher, who watches me silently.

"How are you handling all this?" Asher finally asks.

"Better than I would have thought," I admit. "I took one look at her and I was all-in. There's not a doubt in my mind that I want to be an active part of her life."

"It's a big change. I'm glad you're happy." As the oldest, Asher likes to manage things. I wonder how my brother will handle what I have to say next. "It's a *huge* change… and I'll need my job to adjust with it."

Asher straightens in his seat. In his suit and tie, he reminds me of Linc Kingston, the businessman, even when dealing with family. Then again, he brought Leah a doll she's heard of and it's made her happy. There is a beating heart in there somewhere, I think wryly.

"Meaning what?" Asher asks.

"I want to hire someone to do the traveling when

we have issues at the hotels. Being away and getting a call my daughter was in the hospital? That's not something I want to repeat. I want to be there for everything important." I've been thinking about this the entire plane ride home. "And Aurora? Well, she needs me to have a home base."

Asher's eyes open wide, his expression stunned. "You want to change your entire life for a chick you knocked up over six years ago?"

I stiffen and glance back to make sure Aurora isn't walking down the hall. "Watch it," I warn the brother I respect. "She's not just *some chick*. And she's not just Leah's mother to me, either."

Asher eyes me seriously. "You don't answer to me, Nick. The hotels are your domain. Dad's around, if you need guidance. So am I, but you know more than we do at this point." He crosses one leg over the other. "He groomed you for the hotel business."

I grin. "Because I followed him everywhere, wanting to be just like him." We all have a share in the hotels, but I am the most hands-on.

Asher laughs. "That, I remember. If you want to hire someone to train, then go ahead. Now tell me about Aurora."

Once again, I glance towards the still empty hall, then begin drumming my fingers on the soft sofa. Asher can be trusted with my dark secrets. And I know my brother will love Aurora, too.

"If you think our family has crazy in it, you have no idea what she's been through," I say, keeping my voice low.

Asher raises an eyebrow, waiting.

Although a part of me still hesitates about revealing Aurora's private pain, the only way my family will understand her is if they know. So I spend the next few minutes telling Asher about her past, and explaining the way it is impacting her ability to open up to me now.

"Jesus." Asher rubs his hands together and shakes his head. "Her own parents left her in foster care?" He shakes his head again, his jaw set in anger on her behalf. "No wonder she's got trust issues."

I nod.

Aurora's history beats the story of our mother walking out and never coming back, I think. Not that it's a contest. And my family had our father, Serenity, and each other. I know we were lucky.

But Asher was older, and he remembers our mom…and the neglect. He doesn't like to talk about his childhood, and I respect that.

"You have your hands full right now. I can have my assistant get a list of potential candidates for you to interview."

I nod. "That'll help. Thanks."

"We're family. Whatever you need, I'm here," Asher says. "I just want to make sure you're making this big move because you want it, not because Aurora asked you to."

"Actually, she's never asked. She's admitted that my leaving hits her abandonment issues." I clasp my hands together and lean forward. "I was sitting on the private jet I'd rented at a moment's notice and realized something. Our wealth? We take it for granted. But it enables us to make choices other people can't."

"Like?"

"Like I don't *need* to travel for business. I chose to. Just like I chose not to have a home base, an apartment or a house. Hell, you have homes. Plural," I say.

Asher rises from his seat. "You've grown up a lot in a short time. Gotta say, bro, I'm proud of you."

"Thanks." I stand.

"I need to get going." Asher tips his head towards the entrance. "Tell Aurora I'm sorry I missed her, but that I'd like to get together with you both soon." He starts for the door and pauses. "Fatherhood looks good on you."

I chuckle. "You wait until it's your turn. Fatherhood changes you. *Love* changes you."

Asher shakes his head but says nothing.

I pull my brother into a one-armed hug. "Thanks."

"Anytime."

I let my sibling out and shut the door behind him, then turn…and find Aurora standing at the end of the hall. She's obviously just woken up and stands watching me.

She's showered, and her hair is damp, falling in waves around her face. She wears the same pair of sweats I saw her in that first morning, rolled down and revealing a strip of smooth skin, and a cropped loose short-sleeve top. Her feet are bare, with hot pink toenails.

I love everything about her.

"How are you feeling?" I ask.

"Better. I needed to sleep. Thank you." She rubs her hands together and meets my gaze. "Can we talk?"

No good conversation ever begins with those words, I think, and nod.

Aurora steps towards me and slips her hand into mine, giving me hope that this won't be the doomsday talk I expect.

I follow her into the family room, and when I reach the couch, she places her hands on my shoulders.

"Sit. Please," she says.

I drop to the cushion and settle in, surprised when she climbs into my lap and makes herself comfortable. "What are you doing?"

"Settling in so we can talk." She appears serious,

without any lightheartedness in her expression…but she is sitting *in my lap*.

Her lips purse in the lush pout I like. A lot. I want to kiss those lips, but I know talking is more important. Because I've figured out that she isn't going to drop bad news on me. So I can relax while we work things out.

"You're smiling?" She tips her head to one side, her confusion evident. "Why?"

"Because if you were going to end things between us, you wouldn't be sitting like this." I gesture to our intimate position.

She nods. "You always were smart," she says, leaning down and kissing me. "No," she says, raising her head. "I'm not ending us. But I need to say a few things, and you can decide where we go from here."

"I'm listening."

"I love you, Nick. I've always loved you." Her soft gaze searches my face.

At her admission, my heart picks up speed. "Well, that's great news. Because you already know I love you, too." I tip my head, and she kisses me harder, her mouth warm and willing and she shifts in my lap. A long moan escapes me as her sex comes in contact with my now rock-hard erection. I'm not too comfortable myself, but she raises her head.

"We still need to talk."

Nodding, I hold myself in check. This is her show, and I'll let her lead. "I'm here."

"Melly said some things that resonated with me," she says.

"Like what?" I brace my hands on her hips, holding her in place and just, well, holding her.

"We talked about the choices she had to make when Linc found me in Florida, and how she knew people would talk about her taking in her husband's mistress's pregnant child. And oh, they did talk," she says, shaking her head.

"You heard things?" I tighten my grip on her waist, feeling protective on her behalf.

She nods. "I never told Melly. I didn't think I should say anything to make her feel bad. I knew how fortunate I was—she gave me a home. But Melly told me that she feels like she was the lucky one, that she got so much more than anyone else could understand."

Her eyes fill, and I tighten my hold on her. I'll do anything to take away her pain. I can't change the past, but I can make sure her future is a happy one. And I'm hoping this talk will lead to just that. I hold my breath as I listen.

"She surprised me so much." She swipes under her eyes. "I already knew Melly thinks of Leah as her granddaughter, but I guess I'd never quite grasped that she also considers me her daughter."

That lump rises in my throat all over again.

"She's the only mom I've ever known," Aurora admits, her voice strained.

I rub her back in calming circles, offering comfort…and notice she isn't wearing a bra.

I clear my throat. "Melly's special, and I told her that earlier today."

Aurora blinks. "You did?"

"Baby, you're surrounded by people who are *here*. People who aren't going anywhere. You just need to reach out and take what everyone is offering. What *I'm* offering."

She visibly swallows. "About that. About us…"

I tuck a strand of hair behind her ear and smooth a hand over the long strands.

"Melly asked me, point blank, if I could imagine my life and future without you in it, knowing you'd be there for Leah regardless," Aurora says. "She asked me if I was willing to risk my future because the people in my past let me down."

I know damn well I don't want to imagine my life without Aurora in it. And as more than just my daughter's mother.

I open my mouth, but she places her finger over my lips.

My hand stills on her back, and I meet her gaze.

"So what's the answer?"

She places her hands on either side of my face. "Like I said, I love you, Nick. There is no future for me without you in it. Not one that I want to imagine, anyway. But that doesn't mean I'm not going to have a hard time adjusting. I'm going to have to learn how to get over my abandonment issues. But I'm not sure it's fair to ask you to put up with me as I do it."

I raise an eyebrow. "How about you let me decide what's fair where I'm concerned?" I already know I'll do anything for Aurora and Leah. "If it helps, Asher and I talked about me hiring someone to handle some of the travel."

She shakes her head. "That's not what I want. Changing how you live, your job, what you do? No. I'm going to work on my issues. I just need to know you'll stick by me while I do."

I smile wide. "Just try to get rid of me. And as for cutting down on travel, I think it's still a good idea."

Her eyes gleam with happiness at my reply. She twists her body to face me and wraps her arms around my neck.

"A part of me just wants to make you happy and ease your burdens, but the truth is, not being here when Leah was sick? That was an experience I'd rather not repeat. I've lost so much time with you both already. I don't want to miss any more."

"I understand that." She smooths my cheek with her hand, her eyes twinkling with a lightness I'm thrilled to see. "But I want you to know that if you need to go out of town, or you change your mind and want to go back to the way things are now, I'm not going anywhere. I want to work on myself so I'm a better mother to Leah, a better partner for you and a stronger woman for myself."

"I promise you, we'll make decisions as a team, okay?" I say. "I love the person you are now. If you want to make some changes because you need them, I support you. As far as I'm concerned, you're already one strong woman and an amazing role model to our daughter."

"Yeah?" She rubs her finger over my lips, her eyes dilating with need.

"Definitely. Anything else on the table for discussion? Or can I kiss you without interruption?"

She wraps her arms tighter around my neck and nips at my bottom lip in response. I growl and raise my hips, deliberately coming in contact with her sex. She shifts and archs into me, rubbing herself in circles against my cock.

With my hands on her hips, I help her grind into me, our lips still connected. It's as if I want to be linked with her, forever.

"Mommy, why are you kissing Daddy again?"

Caught again, I think, knowing I need to get used to it.

Aurora slides back but remains on my lap. "Because we love each other." Her eyes sparkle as she answers.

Leah walks over, coughing but sounding much better. "I love you, too." She climbs onto the couch and pushes between us, nearly knocking Aurora over.

Aurora laughs and kisses Leah's forehead. "Kissing is different between mommies and daddies," she says. "But I love you, too."

I tap Leah's head, and she looks up at me. "I love you too, princess."

My daughter flings her arms around my neck. "I love you, Daddy."

My throat tight, I manage to wrap an arm around both of my girls. I have Aurora back. I have my family. And as far as I'm concerned, I have everything that matters.

EPILOGUE

Aurora

One Year Later

I STAND AT the kitchen sink, looking out the window at the rolling backyard of the house Nick I moved into two months ago. When he made the decision to step back from travel, he immediately hired someone who did similar work for a large hotel chain and began the training process. Nick traveled along with his new employee, introducing him to the managers and assistant managers of the hotels, and teaching him the way he likes to handle things under the Meridian umbrella of hotels.

Then he moved in with Leah and me.

Leah has taken to Nick's new living arrangements with ease, acting as if she's always had her father around. And as for me, determined to put my issues in the past, I decided to talk to a therapist about my abandonment issues. Digging up my past is painful, but when I contrast it with my present, I'm finding it easier to trust the happy times will last.

We agreed together to buy a new house, one that is a home for *our* family. Nick loved my house, but as the weather grew warmer, he decided we needed a larger backyard and a pool. He also needs a home office, without taking over mine. My old place had a master and three bedrooms. Leah had one, one was a guestroom, and Nick refused to take over the third one, which I used on occasion for work. After seeing the state of the dining room where he worked before we found this house, I knew he has to have his own office. I would have trouble sharing one with Mr. Messy.

And this new house? I adore it. It's a modern, newly built 10,000 square foot structure at the end of a cul-de-sac, on two acres, with the pool Nick wanted and way too many bedrooms to fill. Excessive? Of course. But once I said I loved it, that was it. Nick wouldn't consider anything else.

Life is so good, I have to pinch myself to believe it's real. I place my hand on my flat belly and smile.

"Are you ready for the savages to arrive?" Nick asks, coming up behind me and wrapping his arms around my waist.

"Is that any way to talk about our families?"

He chuckles. "Maybe not yours, but it definitely fits mine."

I laugh. "It's fine. I'm looking forward to it. Besides, the help you hired to serve and clean have been setting things up in the dining room."

The servers have been coming in and out of the kitchen for the last hour, heating and arranging food and drinks, and setting the tables. Again, it's excessive, but I've discovered that Nick likes his luxuries. And if he can find a way for me to avoid doing housework, or anything beyond working at the charity I love, or spending time with him and Leah, he arranges for things to be done for us.

I'm still not used to being pampered, but there are worse things in life, I think, wryly.

Today is the first time we are having company at the new house—both families. All of the Kingstons and all of the Dares. Jade arrived early and is helping Leah pick out something to wear.

Just as I hoped, Jade and I have become close. I learned the details about Jade's broken engagements. Two men hurt her badly. One proposed but had been using her for her family money, and the most recent one had cheated on her…with his own brother's fiancée. Jade deserves happiness, and I hope she finds someone she can trust. Right now, though, her man-fast continues, and she refuses to let anyone set her up on a blind date. She isn't interested in going out with anyone.

Nick clears his throat. "Hey. Where did you disappear to?" He rests his chin on my shoulder.

"Sorry. I was lost in thought. I'm fine." I turn to him and smile. God, he's sexy. He hasn't shaved because I love his scruff—on his face…and between my thighs. I squirm at the memory of last night. Actually, it's every night, after Leah goes to sleep.

"Before everyone gets here, would you take a walk with me?" he asks.

Taking his hand, I let him lead. He takes me around the gated pool, past the playhouse he transferred here from our old house, beyond the swing set, and walks into the gazebo we put up for shade and relaxation.

He gestures for me to sit, and I lower myself onto the rectangular seat and look up at him. "Why are we out here?" I ask. And why isn't he sitting beside me?

He drops to one knee, and I gasp, realizing he is holding a suede ring box in his hand. "Aurora, I fell in love with you one special night, and in the years after that, I think I was subconsciously waiting for our second chance. I never imagined it would come with a five-year-old sassy girl." He grins, and I want to dive into his arms, but I let him continue.

"I think we've had enough time together as a family for you to be sure. So…" He opens the box revealing an excessively large diamond ring. "Aurora Kingston, will you marry me?"

I blink back tears, managing to nod. "Yes! Yes."

He grins and slides the ring onto my finger. "Thank God. Because this entire day has been planned around you saying yes. From Jade watching our little cockblocker, to all of our families coming soon…"

I glance at the twinkling diamond, afraid to ask how many carats it is. Definitely three or four. The man doesn't know the meaning of the word small.

"Nick," I say, sniffing. "You're too good to me. But there's one more thing you ought to know."

He rises and sits beside me, pulling me into his arms. "Hurry up so I can kiss you senseless."

I meet his gaze. "I'm pregnant."

His eyes open wide, and he presses a hand to my belly. "Jesus. How far along?"

"Not very. We haven't exactly been careful," I remind him.

His grin grows larger. "I haven't exactly minded. Have you been to a doctor?"

I shake my head. "I wanted you to be able to experience every single moment this time."

He presses our lips together, gradually deepening the kiss until we are practically joined and remain that way, devouring each other for a good long while.

When he finally breaks the kiss, he grasps my hands and looks into my eyes. "You're everything I've ever wanted. You and our family."

I blink back tears. "You're everything I was too afraid to dream about."

He takes my hand and pulls me to my feet. "Want to go tell Leah she's going to be a big sister?" he asks, obviously excited.

"You do know she'll tell everyone who walks in the door before we can, right?"

He nods and winks. "That's the point."

Laughing we walk back to the house we call home. It's something I thought I'd never have—a home, a family, and a fiancé I can't live without.

Melly is right. Facing my fears has been difficult, but it's allowed for good things to come. And when things get rough? We'll weather that, too. Together.

Thanks for reading! Jade Dare is next—find out who tempts her to break her man-fast in JUST ONE KISS!

Want even more Carly books?

CARLY'S BOOKLIST by Series – visit:
https://www.carlyphillips.com/CPBooklist

Sign up for Carly's Newsletter:
https://www.carlyphillips.com/CPNewsletter

Join Carly's Corner on Facebook:
https://www.carlyphillips.com/CarlysCorner

Carly on Facebook:
https://www.carlyphillips.com/CPFanpage

Carly on Instagram:
https://www.carlyphillips.com/CPInstagram

Carly's Booklist

newest series listed first

The Sterling Family
Book 1: Just One More Moment (Remington Sterling & Raven Walsh)
Book 2: Just One More Dare (Dex Kingston & Samantha Dare)
Book 3: Just One More Mistletoe (Max Corbin & Brandy Bloom)
Book 4: Just One More Temptation (Fallon Sterling & Noah Powers)
Book 5: Just One More Affair (Jared Sterling & Charlotte Kendall)
Book 6: Just One More Time (Aiden Sterling & Brooke Snyder)
Book 7: Just One More Date (Leo Watson & Camille Hendricks)

The Dirty Dares
Book 1: Just One Dare (Aurora Kingston & Nick Dare)
Book 2: Just One Kiss (Jade Dare & Knox Sinclair)
Book 3: Just One Taste (Asher Dare &

Nicolette Bettencourt)
Book 4: Just One Fling (Harrison Dare &
Winter Capwell)
Book 5: Just One Tease (Zach Dare &
Hadley Stevens)
Novella: Just One Summer (Maddox James &
Gabriella Davenport)

The Kingston Family
Book 1: Just One Night (Linc Kingston &
Jordan Greene)
Book 2: Just One Scandal (Chloe Kingston &
Beck Daniels)
Book 3: Just One Chance (Xander Kingston &
Sasha Keaton)
Book 4: Just One Spark (Dash Kingston &
Cassidy Forrester)
Just Another Spark – Short Story (Dash &
Cassidy revisited)
Novella: Just One Wish (Axel Forrester &
Tara Stillman)

Dare Nation
Book 1: Dare to Resist (Austin Prescott &
Quinn Stone)
Book 2: Dare to Tempt (Damon Prescott &
Evie Wolfe)
Book 3: Dare to Play (Jaxon Prescott & Macy Walker)

Book 4: Dare to Stay (Brandon Prescott &
Willow James)
Novella: Dare to Tease (Hudson Northfield &
Brianne Prescott)

* *Paul Dare's sperm donor kids*

The Sexy Series
Book 1: More Than Sexy (Jason Dare &
Faith Lancaster)
Book 2: Twice As Sexy (Tanner Grayson &
Scarlett Davis)
Book 3: Better Than Sexy (Landon Bennett &
Vivienne Clark)
Novella: Sexy Love (Shane Warden & Amber Davis)

The Knight Brothers
Book 1: Take Me Again (Sebastian Knight &
Ashley Easton)
Novella: Take The Bride (Sierra Knight &
Ryder Hammond)
Book 2: Take Me Down (Parker Knight &
Emily Stevens)
Book 3: Dare Me Tonight (Ethan Knight &
Sienna Dare)
Take Me Now – Short Story (Harper Stevens &
Matt Banks)

The New York Dares

Book 1: Dare to Surrender (Gabe Dare & Isabelle Masters)

Book 2: Dare to Submit (Decklan Dare & Amanda Collins)

Book 3: Dare to Seduce (Max Savage & Lucy Dare)

Dare to Love Series

Book 1: Dare to Love (Ian Dare & Riley Taylor)

Book 2: Dare to Desire (Alex Dare & Madison Evans)

Book 3: Dare to Touch (Dylan Rhodes & Olivia Dare)

Book 4: Dare to Hold (Scott Dare & Meg Thompson)

Book 5: Dare to Rock (Avery Dare & Grey Kingston)

Book 6: Dare to Take (Tyler Dare & Ella Shaw)

A Very Dare Christmas – Short Story (Ian & Riley revisited)

* *Sienna Dare gets together with Ethan Knight in* **The Knight Brothers** *(Dare Me Tonight).*

* *Jason Dare gets together with Faith in the* **Sexy Series** *(More Than Sexy).*

* *Kaden Barnes (you met him at the end of Dare to Take) has his own book in* **The Billionaire Bad Boys** *(Going Down Easy).*

For the most recent Carly books, visit CARLY'S BOOKLIST page

www.carlyphillips.com/CPBooklist

Other Indie Series

Billionaire Bad Boys
Book 1: Going Down Easy (Kaden Barnes & Lexie Parker)
Book 2: Going Down Fast (Lucas Monroe & Maxie Sullivan)
Book 3: Going Down Hard (Derek West & Cassie Storms)
Book 4: Going In Deep (Julian Dane & Kendall Parker)
Going Down Again – Short Story (Kade & Lexie revisited)

Bodyguard Bad Boys
Book 1: Rock Me (Ben Hollander & Summer Michelle)
Book 2: Tempt Me (Austin Rhodes & Mia Atwood)
Novella: His To Protect (Talia Shaw & Shane Landon)

Serendipity Series
Book 1: Serendipity (Ethan Barron & Faith Harrington)
Book 2: Kismet (Lissa Gardelli & Trevor Dane)
Book 3: Destiny (Nash Barron & Kelly Moss)
Book 4: Fated (Kate Andrews & Nick Mancini)
Book 5: Karma (Dare Barron & Liza McKnight)

Serendipity's Finest

Book 1: Perfect Fit (Michael Marsden & Cara Hartley)

Book 2: Perfect Fling (Erin Marsden & Cole Sanders)

Book 3: Perfect Together (Sam Marsden & Nicole Farnsworth)

Book 4: Perfect Strangers (Alexa Collins & Luke Thompson)

Hot Heroes Series

Book 1: Touch You Now (Halley Ward & Kane Harmon)

Book 2: Hold You Now (Phoebe Ward & Jake Nichols)

Book 3: Need You Now (Juliette Collins & Braden Clark)

Book 4: Want You Now (Andi Harmon & Kyle Davenport)

The Chandler Brothers

Book 1: The Bachelor (Roman Chandler & Charlotte Bronson)

Book 2: The Playboy (Rick Chandler & Kendall Sutton)

Book 3: The Heartbreaker (Chase Chandler & Sloane Carlisle)

The Lucky Series

Book 1: Lucky Charm (Derek Corwin &

Gabrielle Donovan)

Book 2: Lucky Streak (Mike Corwin& Amber
Rose Brennan)

Book 3: Lucky Break (Jason Corwin &
Lauren Perkins)

Costas Sisters

Book 1: Under the Boardwalk (Ariana Costas &
Quinn Donovan)

Book 2: Summer of Love (Zoe Costas &
Ryan Baldwin)

Ty and Hunter

Book 1: Cross My Heart (Lilly Dumont & Ty Benson)

Book 2: Sealed with a Kiss (Molly Gifford &
Daniel Hunter)

The Hot Zone

Book 1: Hot Stuff (Annabelle Jordan &
Brandon Vaughn)

Book 2: Hot Number (Micki Jordan & Damian Fuller)

Book 3: Hot Item (Sophie Jordan & Riley Nash)

Book 4: Hot Property (Amy Stone & John Roper)

The Simply Series

Book 1: Simply Sinful (Kayla Luck &
Kane McDermott)

Book 2: Simply Scandalous (Catherine Luck &

Logan Montgomery)
Book 3: Simply Sensual (Ben Callahan &
Grace Montgomery)
Book 4: Body Heat (Jake Lowell & Brianne Nelson)
Book 5: Simply Sexy (Rina Lowell & Colin Lyons)

The Most Eligible Bachelor Series
Book 1: Kiss Me if You Can (Sam Cooper &
Lexie Davis)
Book 2: Love Me If You Dare (Rafe Mancuso &
Sara Rios)

Carly Classics
Book 1: The Right Choice (Carly Wexler &
Mike Novak)
Book 2: Perfect Partners (Chelsie Russell &
Griffin Stuart)
Book 3: Unexpected Chances (Dylan North &
Holly Evans)
Book 4: Worthy of Love (Kevin Manning &
Nikki Welles)

For the most recent Carly books, visit CARLY'S
BOOKLIST page
www.carlyphillips.com/CPBooklist

Carly's Still Traditionally Published Books

Stand-Alone Books

The Seduction – Kindle Worlds, The Arrangement Universe – No Longer Available

More Than Words Volume 7 – Compassion

Can't Wait

Naughty Under the Mistletoe

Grey's Anatomy 101 Essay

For the most recent Carly books, visit CARLY'S BOOKLIST page

www.carlyphillips.com/CPBooklist

About the Author

NY Times, Wall Street Journal, and USA Today Bestseller, Carly Phillips is the queen of Alpha Heroes, at least according to The Harlequin Junkie Reviewer. Carly married her college sweetheart and lives in Purchase, NY along with her crazy dogs who are featured on her Facebook and Instagram pages. The author of over 75 romance novels, she has raised two incredible daughters and is now an empty nester. Carly's book, The Bachelor, was chosen by Kelly Ripa as her first romance club pick. Carly loves social media and interacting with her readers. Want to keep up with Carly? Sign up for her newsletter and receive TWO FREE books at www.carlyphillips.com.

www.ingramcontent.com/pod-product-compliance
Lightning Source LLC
Chambersburg PA
CBHW071239190726
48292CB00007B/2356